These girls are on the adventure of their lives. But with teamwork and their own special abilities, they just might be Cayenga Park's newest heroes . . .

girls R.U.L.E.

Kayla Adams's wavy brown hair and dark, almond-shaped eyes attract attention, but her quick temper and sharp tongue keep it— especially when she stands up for her friends.

Carson McDonald has never let her hearing disability get in her way. In fact, it has forced this blonde, beautiful athlete to be extra- sensitive to her environment—qualities which make her an excel- lent sleuth.

Becca Fisher is a natural clown, always cracking jokes. But her sarcastic sense of humor often has a way of getting the petite, wiry girl with deep green eyes in trouble.

Sophie Schultz is intense, determined, and stubborn. Nicknamed "little bulldog" by her dad, this redhead knows what she wants and goes after it despite all obstacles, including her older brother and junior ranger, Kyle!

Alex Loomis-Drake has a million facts stored in her head, and a million interests to match. But although this girl with brown, silky hair comes from a wealthy family, she isn't your usual pampered princess.

Don't miss any of the girls R.U.L.E. adventures!

girls R.U.L.E.

#2

TRAIL OF TERROR

Kris Lowe

BERKLEY JAM BOOKS, NEW YORK

GIRLS R.U.L.E.: TRAIL OF TERROR

A Berkley Jam Book / published by arrangement with
the author

PRINTING HISTORY
Berkley Jam edition / October 1998

The Penguin Putnam Inc. World Wide Web site address is
http://www.penguinputnam.com

ISBN: 0-425-16620-1

BERKLEY JAM BOOKS®
Berkley Jam Books are published by The Berkley Publishing Group,
a member of Penguin Putnam Inc.,
375 Hudson Street, New York, New York 10014.
BERKLEY JAM and its logo are trademarks
belonging to Berkley Publishing Corporation.

PRINTED IN THE UNITED STATES OF AMERICA

10 9 8 7 6 5 4 3 2 1

To Alexandra, Amanda, Elizabeth, Emily, Georgia, Julia, Kaitlin H., Kaitlin P., Kathryn, Madeline, Maya, Nella, Sara, Stefi, Sylvia . . . and Fiona, of course.

girls R.U.L.E.

#2

TRAIL OF TERROR

SOPHIE

ONE

A note was taped to the assignment board outside the Cayenga Park Headquarters building. I squinted in the California sunshine to read it.

JUNIOR RANGERS—

PLEASE SEE ME ABOUT TODAY'S PARK

ASSIGNMENTS.

—RANGER ABE MAYFIELD

"I wonder what that's about?" asked Becca Fisher, who was standing beside me.

Becca and I had just started out as members of GIRLS

R.U.L.E., the new girls' division of the park's Ranger Unit Learning Extension. There are five of us in the division: Becca, Kayla, Alex, Carson, and me.

I shrugged. "Only one way to find out," I replied.

Becca and I headed into the building and made our way through the meeting room to Ranger Abe's office. Inside, we found Ranger Abe leaning against his desk, talking to Kayla and Alex. Kayla and Alex go to the same school, Harmon Academy, so they usually head over to the park together on the afternoons when we're on duty. Becca, Carson, and I go to Cayenga High School.

It was Kayla who came up with the idea for the five of us to call ourselves GIRLS R.U.L.E., since that's what the initials of Ranger Unit Learning Extension spell out. I loved the name as soon as I heard it. And I was starting to love being a junior ranger, too.

Which kind of surprised me, to tell the truth. You see, the only reason I even took the junior ranger test to begin with was to prove to my brother, Jason, that I could do it. Jason's in the boys' division of the junior rangers. When the park decided to create the girls' division, Jason and a few of the other guys started going around making obnoxious comments about how no girl could ever pass the test. I decided to try to prove they were wrong.

What I hadn't realized was how much I was going to like being a ranger. But working outside is great. And I get to meet people from all over the world who come to visit the park. On top of that, the other four members of GIRLS R.U.L.E. are turning out to be some of my best friends ever.

Ranger Abe nodded when he saw Becca and me come into the office. "Hello, girls. I'm glad you're here. Isn't Carson with you?"

I shook my head. "She had to talk to her track coach about something. But she said she'd be over in a few minutes." Carson is on about a million teams at school. She's totally athletic.

Ranger Abe nodded. "Well, I can fill her in when she gets here."

Kayla's amber eyes looked serious. "So what's going on, Ranger Abe? Is there some kind of problem in the park?"

"There may be," Ranger Abe responded. "We've been asked by the authorities to keep an eye out for anything suspicious near the reservoir."

"The reservoir?" Becca repeated. "Why?"

"A sample from the reservoir came close to failing a safe water test this morning," Ranger Abe explained. "There were trace amounts of a chemical found in it."

"What kind of chemical?" Alex asked, smoothing a lock of her straight brown hair behind her ear. Alex knows a lot about chemicals and stuff. She's totally into science and math.

Ranger Abe shook his head. "I'm not sure. In any case, there wasn't enough of whatever it was in the water to actually be dangerous. But it was unusual. The authorities have asked that all park workers keep an eye out for any strange behavior from park visitors, or anything odd on the trails or near the streams."

"The streams?" I repeated. "But I thought the problem was in the reservoir."

"The streams feed directly into the reservoir," Ranger Abe explained. "And the reservoir feeds directly into the town of Cayenga's drinking water supply."

"Wow," I said. This sounded like it could be serious. I'd never really thought about where the water I drank came from before. I definitely didn't like the idea of drinking chemicals.

"Okay, Ranger Abe, sure thing," Kayla said, her mass of brown braids bobbing as she nodded. "We'll keep an eye out and report anything we find."

"Do you want us to go straight to the trails and check things out?" Alex asked.

"I think that's a good idea," Ranger Abe agreed. "While you're there you can check out the trail markers. We've had several reports of visitors getting lost on the trails by Mesa del Oro and the reservoir in the past few weeks."

"Few weeks, huh? I guess they sure will be glad to see us when we find them," Becca cracked.

I laughed. Becca has a really great sense of humor. She's always joking about something.

Ranger Abe smiled. "Sure, let me know if you find anyone, Becca," he said with a chuckle. "Okay then, Kayla and Sophie, why don't you take the blue trail. Alex and Becca can take the red trail, and when Carson gets here, I'll send her to the green trail. And remember, keep your eyes open for anything unusual."

Twenty minutes later, Kayla and I stopped at a fork in the blue trail.

"Which way do we go now?" Kayla wondered out loud.

I stopped beside her and stared at the path ahead of us. Each of the two paths led off in a different direction through the woods. There were no signs, no trail markers, nothing.

I blew a lock of my curly red hair off my forehead. "Beats me," I answered.

"Let's check the trail map," Kayla suggested.

"Oh right, the map," I responded, laughing a little. "Good idea." I pulled my trail map out of the back pocket of my frayed cutoffs.

I unfolded the map, and Kayla and I studied it together.

After a moment I gave up on the map, handed it to Kayla, and glanced around again. I'm not really the map type. Sitting still and concentrating aren't exactly my strongest qualities.

"It looks like the blue trail leads north," Kayla murmured, her eyes still on the map. "I guess I should check my compass." She dug in the pocket of her brown corduroy pants.

I wandered over to the spot where the path split. I spotted a small, squared-off wooden signpost lying in the grass. I recognized it as the kind that was used to mark the trails.

"Hey, look at this! It must have fallen over," I called. I turned to Kayla, but she was still studying the map and compass.

I picked up the signpost. Sure enough, a faded blue spot on one side of the post showed that it was a marker for the blue trail.

But which way is this supposed to go? I wondered. I stuck

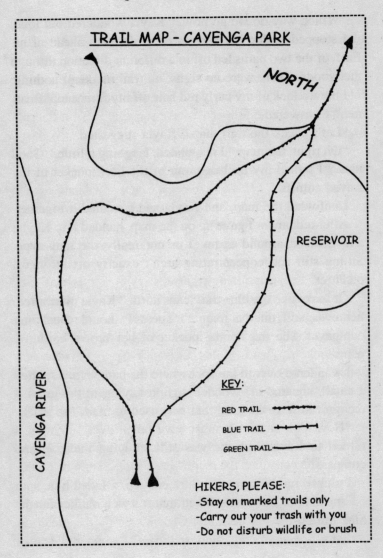

TRAIL MAP – CAYENGA PARK

NORTH

RESERVOIR

CAYENGA RIVER

KEY:

RED TRAIL •••••••••
BLUE TRAIL ++++++++
GREEN TRAIL ————

HIKERS, PLEASE:
-Stay on marked trails only
-Carry out your trash with you
-Do not disturb wildlife or brush

the stick in the ground and rotated it from side to side. The blue spot could mark either the right or the left fork of the trail, depending on how I positioned it.

"North should be to our right," Kayla said, still looking intently at the map. "But I can't find this fork in the path on the map anywhere. It doesn't make sense. It's like it doesn't exist."

"Tell that to the trail," I joked. I looked around. "No wonder people have been getting lost out here." Then I spotted something on a tree to my left. It was a small, square piece of wood, nailed to the trunk just above the level of my head. I walked over to it.

The wood was old and weathered, but I could still make out a yellow shape painted on it.

"Hey!" I said, realizing what it was. "A horseshoe!"

Kayla walked over to look at it. "I wonder what that means. I guess this could be a marker for a horse trail. But I've never seen any horses in the park, have you?"

I shook my head. "I bet Carson can tell us what it's about," I said. Carson knows her way around the park better than anyone else in GIRLS R.U.L.E. Her mom works as a Cayenga Park ranger, so Carson practically grew up in the park.

"Let's ask her about it when we meet up with her," Kayla agreed. She consulted the map. "She's supposed to be on the green trail, right?"

I nodded, remembering Ranger Abe's words. "Becca and Alex are on the red trail, and Carson's doing the green on her own."

"I think we should keep right," Kayla decided. "We know that way is north, and that's where the trail is supposed to take us. According to the map, the three trails connect. If we're on track, we should meet up with Becca, Alex, and Carson just past the reservoir."

"Sounds good to me," I replied. Actually, I wasn't following the details of what Kayla was saying very closely. Like I said, I'm not that great with maps and directions.

We continued through the woods. A few moments later the trail came out beside a small stream. Kayla suddenly stopped short.

"What is it?" I asked her. "Isn't this the right way?"

"Just look at that!" Kayla pointed toward the stream. Her amber eyes were flashing with anger.

I looked down in the direction she was pointing. Lying in the water at the side of the stream were several rusty soda cans, an empty bag of potato chips, two candy wrappers, and a plastic six-pack holder.

"Yuck," I said, staring at the mess. Then I thought of something. "Oh, wow, do you think this could have anything to do with the water problem Ranger Abe told us about?"

"I don't know," Kayla replied. "He said it was a chemical they found in the water, didn't he?"

"Yeah," I said. "I guess regular, ordinary old garbage probably wouldn't have much to do with that."

"Still, we'd better do something about this," Kayla decided. She shook her head. "How can people be so dumb?

Don't they realize that this stuff can be dangerous for wildlife?"

"We should definitely report it," I agreed.

Kayla pulled her green Cayenga Park baseball cap off her head and squatted down by the edge of the stream. She picked up the plastic six-pack holder. "This is terrible! Ducks and beavers and other animals get caught in these things." She sighed and started piling the dirty trash into her baseball cap.

I stared at her in astonishment. "Kayla! Your hat!"

"I can't just leave all this stuff here," Kayla replied. "And I don't have anything else to carry it in."

That's one of the things I love about Kayla. She's always ready to do whatever it takes to stand behind what she thinks is right. A lot of people say they're for protecting animals or keeping the environment clean. But Kayla's probably the only person I know who would voluntarily put a bunch of wet garbage into her hat to clean up a stream.

I bent down beside her and picked up a couple of cans and a candy wrapper. *I guess it's kind of a lucky break that I don't have my hat with me today,* I admitted secretly to myself. *Seeing what Kayla is doing probably would have made me feel like I should do the same. I only have one Cayenga Park hat, and I'm not even sure if they're washable!*

After Kayla and I had collected the garbage, we continued down the trail, Kayla carrying her dripping hat in her hands.

As we passed the reservoir on our right, I looked at the

water. Gazing out over the sparkling blue surface of the reservoir, I remembered what Ranger Abe had said about the park's streams feeding into the reservoir, and the reservoir feeding into the town's water supply. I realized I was really glad that Kayla had stopped by that stream so we could pick up the garbage.

A few moments after we passed the reservoir I heard a familiar voice from among some nearby trees.

"Hi, Sophie! Hi, Kayla!"

I turned and saw someone in a bright orange tank top and baggy black pants waving to us from a path just beyond the trees. It was Becca, and with her was Alex.

I returned the wave. "Hi, you guys."

"I think our two trails meet just ahead," Alex called. "Let's all keep going and find out."

We continued walking. Sure enough, a few moments later, Alex and Becca appeared just ahead of us. Kayla and I joined them.

"Phew!" Becca wiped her short, silky dark hair off her forehead. "I'm glad we made it out of that wilderness alive!" She rolled her eyes, pretending to look relieved.

The rest of us laughed. Becca's from New York. She's always kidding around about being a city girl, and calling the park a wilderness or a jungle.

"Actually, following the trail wasn't as easy as I expected," Alex agreed, her shoulder-length brown ponytail bobbing as she nodded her head. "There were several trail markers missing or broken; I'd estimate about twenty percent of them in all."

Alex is totally logical. And smart. *If Alex had trouble following the trail, it's no wonder park visitors have been getting lost,* I realized.

Then Alex noticed the dripping garbage in Kayla's hat. "Hey, what's all that?" she asked with concern in her big, brown eyes.

Kayla held out her hat, and the expression of disgust returned to her face. "Cans, wrappers, and other junk I took out of the stream."

"Wait a minute, Kayla, don't you know it's against park rules for hikers to gather souvenirs from the park landscape?" Becca joked.

I saw Kayla smile in spite of herself. "I wish more hikers would take *this* kind of souvenir with them," she said with a sigh.

"We were wondering if this stuff could have anything to do with the chemical in the water Ranger Abe told us about," I explained.

Alex shook her head. "Probably not. But it's good you guys picked it up. And you should definitely report it anyway."

"Hey, look," Becca said suddenly. "There's Carson up ahead."

Walking in the distance on the path ahead of us was a familiar figure with a blonde braid, dressed in white shorts and a blue and white Cayenga High Varsity Volleyball T-shirt.

I drew in my breath to call out her name. But then I stopped, remembering. Carson has a hearing disability. She has no hearing at all in one ear, and only some hearing in the other. Carson explained to all of us when we first started working together that she needs to use stuff she can *see* to help her make up for the stuff she doesn't *hear*. For example, she reads lips to help her understand what people are saying. *Calling out to her from behind is definitely not the best way to get Carson's attention,* I realized.

"Come on, let's catch up to her," I suggested instead.

The four of us picked up our pace and started to run down the trail. To my surprise, Carson turned around almost immediately.

"Hi, guys," she said with a smile as we caught up to her. "I thought that must be you."

I stared at her in surprise. "But how did you know we were coming?"

"I felt the vibration in the ground from your running." She laughed a little. "You guys aren't exactly light on your feet, you know. Except for Becca, that is," she added.

"That's because *my* feet are filled with helium," Becca joked. She flipped into a handstand, her sandaled feet high in the air, and took a few steps with her hands. I shook my head in amazement. Becca studied gymnastics for years back in New York. She can do stuff with her body that I probably wouldn't even try in my dreams.

"Anyway," Carson went on, "I knew it must be either you guys behind me or a herd of wild horses about to mow me down."

We all laughed.

"Hey, speaking of horses," I said, remembering the sign I'd seen, "are there any horses anywhere in the park?"

"Yeah, I think so," Carson said. "I'm pretty sure there's one ranch left, over in the Mill Valley area of the park."

"*Left?* What do you mean?" Kayla asked.

"From what my mom tells me, horseback riding used to be pretty popular in the park," Carson explained. "When she first started working as a ranger, there were three or four ranches here, I think, and lots of horse trails."

"I guess that explains that sign we saw back in the woods, Sophie," Kayla said.

"Kayla and I found an old marker with a horseshoe on it nailed to a tree near the blue trail," I explained to the others.

"We saw one of those, too," Becca said excitedly.

"Probably from some old horse trails for visitors," Carson agreed. "Although visitors weren't the only ones who used to ride in the park. My mother told me that some of the rangers even used to patrol the park on horseback."

"Wow, that sounds fun," I said appreciatively.

I thought back to the one time I'd ever been on a horse. It was when I was little, when my dad still lived with us. One day he'd taken me to a county fair outside of town, near some farmland. I remember it was just me and my dad. I don't remember where my brother and my mom were that day. But I know it felt really special to just be with my dad. There was a pony ride at the fair, and he bought me a ticket for it. At first I was really scared sitting up there in that saddle by myself. I felt like I'd made a big mistake. But I wasn't about to turn back. Then the pony started to walk around the ring, and soon I began to enjoy it. By the time the ride was over I was having a great time. My dad let me ride four more times that day.

Becca's voice broke into my thoughts. "How come the rangers don't ride anymore, Carson?"

Carson shrugged.

"Probably because it's a lot more efficient to use jeeps and mountain bikes," Alex pointed out.

"Still, I think riding a horse around in the park sounds like way more fun," I said.

Alex groaned. "That's because your parents didn't make you take riding lessons at the Cayenga Heights Country Club. Believe me, it was awful. I lasted about three days. I'd rather patrol the park on a bike any day."

"You'd rather do *anything* on a bike, Alex," Kayla pointed out. Alex is totally into mountain biking. She even built her own mountain bike.

"Yeah," Becca said with a grin. "I bet you even sleep on a bike. Do you actually have a bed in your room? Or is it just a bike with a pillow and a blanket?"

We all laughed.

"Well, I still say you're lucky you got to learn how to ride," I said wistfully. "I'd love to take riding lessons."

"So why don't you?" Carson asked.

"Where?" I asked. "My family doesn't belong to any clubs with riding. Come to think of it, my family doesn't belong to any clubs, period." I laughed. "Unless you count our membership at Video-to-Go."

Becca laughed. "Good one, Sophie."

"I'm serious, Sophie," Carson said. "If you really want to learn how to ride, why don't you go check out that ranch over in the Mill Valley part of the park."

"Do you think they give lessons?" I asked.

Carson shrugged. "They might."

"Only one way to find out," Alex pointed out.

"Yeah, Sophie, you should go for it," Kayla urged.

"Maybe I will," I decided. The more I thought about it, the more I liked the idea. I could learn to ride right here in the park. Then maybe I could even persuade Ranger Abe to let me patrol on horseback sometimes, like the rangers used to.

There was another reason I wanted to learn how to ride. You see, Kayla, Becca, Alex, and Carson each had something they were really good at, something that helped them be even better junior rangers. Alex was an incredible biker and really smart, and Becca had her gymnastics skills. Kayla had been studying karate for years at her father's martial arts school. And Carson was an amazing athlete, the captain of a bunch of teams at Cayenga High. If I learned how to ride, then I'd have a special way to help out in the park, too.

I made up my mind to check out the ranch in Mill Valley the first chance I got.

TWO

Later that evening I watched as my brother hacked away at a cucumber with a butter knife.

"Jason, you're making a total mess out of that," I said. "Get a sharper knife."

"There isn't one," he answered without looking up.

"That's ridiculous," I told him as I rinsed off a tomato. "Just go look in the drawer."

"You go look," he replied.

I sighed. Jason can be such a pain sometimes. We were supposed to be making a salad together for dinner, but so far I'd done most of the work. Not that I should have been surprised. Somehow that seems to happen whenever Jason and I are supposed to help out around the house together. He must be the only fifteen-year-old boy in the world who is actually allergic to chores.

When I got back to the counter, I saw that Jason was using the knife I had taken out to use on the tomato.

"Hey, that's my knife," I said.

"Is not," he responded.

"Is too," I insisted.

Just then the kitchen door opened, and my mother came in. She was dressed in the blue and white uniform she wears for her job as an aide at the Cayenga County Hospital, and she was carrying a bundle of mail.

"Mom," I complained, "Jason took my knife!"

"It's not just your knife," Jason retorted. "I can use it if I want."

My mother sighed. "Can't you two stop? This isn't exactly what I was hoping to come home to after a long day of work."

I felt bad. I knew my mom must be tired. I walked over to the silverware drawer and silently took out another knife. Jason stuck his tongue out at me. I crossed my eyes at him.

My mother sat down at the kitchen table and started going through the mail. "Did anybody start the pasta water?" she asked.

Jason dropped his knife on the counter with a clatter. "I have to make a phone call. Tell me when dinner's ready, okay?"

"Mom!" I complained as Jason ran out of the room.

But my mother didn't answer. She was busy examining the mail.

"Mom," I tried again.

My mother glanced up from the mail, a preoccupied

expression on her face. "Sophie," she said, "boil some water for the pasta, would you?"

I sighed and took a pot out of the cabinet. I filled it with water and put it on the stove to boil and finished cutting the tomato. Then I sat down at the table with my mother.

"Hey, Mom, can I talk to you about something?" I asked.

"Mmmmm," she answered without looking up.

"I was thinking I might like to take horseback riding lessons," I said. "There's this place in the park that Carson told me about—"

"Oh, honey," my mother cut me off. As she looked at me her face seemed sad. "That sounds so nice. But I'm afraid we really can't afford it."

"Oh." My heart sank at her words.

"I'd love to be able to get you kids extras like lessons and things," my mother went on. She held up a couple of pieces of mail. "But it's all I can do to meet these bills on my salary as it is."

What about Dad? I wanted to ask. *Isn't he supposed to help pay for stuff for us?* But I knew better than to say anything. I'd heard my mom on the phone with my dad a few times lately, arguing about money. I knew it was probably a sensitive subject. Besides, I didn't want to get her started talking about my dad. I mean, I knew she was upset about the way he'd moved out on us and everything, but I still hated to hear my mom say anything bad about him.

I felt a tightening in my throat.

"I hope you understand, Sophie," my mother said gently.

"Yeah, sure. No big deal," I managed, my voice low. I started out of the room. When I felt this way, only one thing could make me feel better—music. I just wanted to get up to my room and put on my new CD, the latest by the Hot Potatoes.

"Sophie?" my mom called after me. "Don't go too far. Dinner will be ready soon."

"Call me," I replied, starting up the stairs.

Two days later I sat in the meeting room at Park Headquarters along with the other members of GIRLS R.U.L.E. as well as Jason and the rest of the boys' division. It was Saturday morning, time for our regular weekly meeting with Ranger Abe.

Ranger Abe stood in front of us, a clipboard in his hand. "All right then, let's start by going over the business of the past week," he said. "I know you're all aware that we had a little problem with the reservoir water the other day when the girls were on duty."

Rick Neely, the sixteen-year-old unofficial head of the boys' division, let out a little laugh. "That figures," he said. "There never would have been any problem at all if us guys had been on duty that day."

Ranger Abe shot him a stern look. "It so happens that the water problem occurred *before* the girls came to work that day," he said. "The girls were only involved because I asked them to keep an eye out for anything unusual on the trails. But, other than a bit of garbage, no one saw anything out of place, isn't that right, girls?"

Kayla nodded and raised her hand. "How has the reservoir water been since then, Ranger Abe?"

"I'm happy to say everything seems just find now," Ranger Abe replied. "Whatever the problem was, it apparently cleared up a day or two later." He consulted his clipboard. "Now, girls, you were going to inspect the trail markers around Mesa del Oro and the reservoir. How did that go?"

"There were a lot of missing markers on all the trails," Alex volunteered. "I can see why visitors might be having trouble following them."

I raised my hand. "A couple of the trails also meet up with some old horse trails that aren't even on the map," I explained. "That's probably confusing people, too."

Ranger Abe nodded. "Thanks, girls. We'll have to think of a way to take care of that." He checked the clipboard again and turned toward two of the guys in the boys' division. "Walker and Chris, you were going to repaint the float over at the cove beach, isn't that right?"

Walker, a tall, slim African-American guy with closely cropped hair, nodded. "We got it done. The float should be ready to go back in the water today."

"Good work." Ranger Abe turned back to his clipboard. "All right then, let's get to today's assignments, and then on to the rest of the week. I need two lifeguards for the kiddie beach. Kevin and Rick? How about you?"

Rick let out a groan. "The *kiddie* beach? Oh, come on, Ranger Abe. Use the girls for the kiddie beach and give me something better. You know, tougher, something right for me."

"If you ask me, the *kiddie* beach is exactly where you belong, Rick," Becca muttered.

I stifled a laugh. I know Ranger Abe really wants us to try to get along, but I just love it when Becca gives Rick what he deserves. Rick is definitely the most obnoxious guy in the junior rangers, probably even the most obnoxious guy at Cayenga High. He's also my brother Jason's best friend.

"Sorry, Rick, but that's where we need you today," Ranger Abe replied. He checked his clipboard again. "Now, I'd like to start working on fixing up those trails. Girls, since you know the problem well, why don't you head up there and start replacing those markers. I've got some extra stakes and some paint in the office I can give you."

Alex raised her hand. "What about the horse trails? Do you want us to close those off in some way so they won't confuse people?"

Ranger Abe shook his head. "I don't think we can. Technically, they're still open for use."

I sat up in surprise at his words. "Really?"

"But no one ever rides on them," Carson pointed out.

"Not much anymore, it's true," Ranger Abe agreed. "But as long as there's still a ranch operated within the park's boundaries we've got to keep them open. Officially the horse trails don't even come under park jurisdiction, since the ranches that originally set them up and used them were all privately owned. I do see what you mean about their being confusing for hikers, though."

"Maybe it would help if the park's trail maps showed something about where the horse trails are, too," Kayla suggested.

Ranger Abe nodded. "Good idea. We're due to have more trail maps printed up soon anyway. Maybe we should add some notes about where the horse trails meet up with the hiking trails." He thought a moment. "In fact, there used to be a map that the ranchers gave out to riders. It was just an old hand-drawn thing, but I bet it would help us out. Maybe a couple of you should head over to the ranch in Mill Valley and see if the old couple who run the place, the Flynns, have any copies left of that."

My hand shot up right away. "I'll go, Ranger Abe." Even though my mom had said no to the riding lessons, I was eager to see the ranch and the horses for myself.

Ranger Abe nodded. "All right, Sophie, that would be fine. Becca, you can go with her. When you get back you can join the rest of your division on the trails." He turned back to his clipboard. "Now, I need two more junior rangers to fix a hole in the fence around the reservoir. Jason? Walker?"

THREE

Twenty minutes later Becca and I were hiking along the Cayenga River toward Mill Valley. The sun was hot on my back, and the cool air from the river felt good. Looking at the sparkling water, I remembered what Kayla had told me the other day.

"A lot of the streams around here feed into the town reservoir," I told Becca. "I wonder if the river does, too."

Becca shook her head. "You're asking the wrong person, Sophie. I'm not exactly an expert on the geography of Cayenga Park. Now, *Central* Park in New York is another story." She grinned.

I smiled, too. "What's New York like, anyway? Is it really exciting?" I've always thought that I'd love to visit New York. I've heard it has a totally cool music scene.

Becca shrugged. "I guess, if you're a tourist. To me it's

just my hometown. It's very different from here, though. I mean, there's a lot more to do in New York than there is in Cayenga. But Cayenga's nice in a different way. Still, it was hard for me to get used to at first. People here seem kind of old-fashioned sometimes."

"Old-fashioned?" I said with surprise. "What do you mean?"

"You know," Becca replied, "like they're shocked pretty easily by stuff."

"Oh," I said, realizing what Becca was probably talking about. You see, Becca doesn't exactly look like the typical Cayenga High student. Or, she might, if it weren't for the little silver nose ring she wears in her left nostril. When Becca first started school, a lot of people definitely thought she was weird because of her nose ring.

Not me, though. One of my favorite singers, Alyssa Raith, has a pierced nose. I only wish I had the guts to get something like that. Even if I did, though, my mother would probably go nuts.

"I guess it's just that some stuff that seems normal in New York isn't what people here are used to," I said to Becca.

"I guess," she agreed. Then she looked around at the landscape and smiled. "Anyway, Central Park definitely doesn't compare to this."

I gazed around. I had never been in this exact part of the park before. It wasn't an area that visitors used frequently, either. There were no real hiking and biking trails down here by this part of the river, and no campgrounds, either. But it was definitely beautiful. The grass along the riverbank was green and lush, and we were surrounded by majestic, tree-covered mountains.

"I guess we should be there soon," I told Becca. "Ranger Abe said all we had to do was follow the river and it would lead straight into the valley."

"Hey," Becca exclaimed, pointing upriver, "what's that?"

Ahead of us, perched on the riverbank, stood a large barn-shaped building.

"Maybe it's the ranch," I guessed. "Do you think we're in the valley now?"

"Beats me," Becca replied. "Let's check it out."

But as we approached the building, I began to doubt that it was the ranch. The building, which was made of wood, was sagging almost into the river in places. Its deep red paint was peeling, and there were several boards missing from the outside walls.

"It looks pretty old," I said to Becca. "It seems like it's falling apart."

"I wonder what it is," Becca said, "or *was*."

Together, we walked around the building. The side of the structure that faced the mountains was even more damaged than the side near the river. Most of the exterior boards were missing or splintered. Becca and I peered between the bare wooden struts supporting the building.

Inside was a huge dark space. Something fluttered near the rafters. Becca and I glanced at each other and backed away from the building. Despite the warm sunshine, I felt a small chill go down my spine.

"Do you think those were bats?" Becca asked a little nervously.

"I don't know," I replied. "But if they were, they won't hurt us. Come on, let's look around the other side."

Together, Becca and I walked through the grass to the upstream side of the building.

"Wow, look at that!" Becca said.

A huge wooden wheel sat against the building just above the surface of the water. At the end of each of the wheel's spokes was a wooden paddle. Directly above the wheel was what looked like an old, wooden slide of some kind. Water was running out of the slide and into the river. To one side of the wheel was a faded, peeling sign.

```
┌─────────────────────────────────┐
│  ┌───────────────────────────┐  │
│  │   CLARK PAPER MILL        │  │
│  └───────────────────────────┘  │
└─────────────────────────────────┘
```

"Hey, this must be it," I said.

"The ranch?" Becca said doubtfully.

"No, the mill," I replied. "The *mill*. You know, where Mill Valley gets its name. This must have once been a real paper mill."

"You mean like a factory? In the middle of the park?" Becca said. "That doesn't make sense."

"I guess not," I agreed. Then I had an idea. "But maybe it was back before the park *was* a park."

"When was that?" Becca asked.

I shrugged. "Who knows? But it must have been made into a park *some*time, right?"

"Beats me," Becca replied. "All I know is that the more I learn about the park the more I realize I *don't* know about the park."

Just then, I was startled by the sound of voices from above us.

"Someone's on the mountain up there," I said.

We backed up a bit and craned our necks. About thirty feet up on the side of the nearest mountain, a man and a woman were standing on a trail. They had set up a tripod, like the kind photographers set their cameras on. The woman was peering through what looked like the lens of the camera and talking to the man. Her voice echoed off the mountains, but I couldn't hear what she was saying. The man seemed to be taking notes on a clipboard.

"I guess they're photographers or something," I decided. "Come on, let's keep going. The ranch must be pretty close now."

Sure enough, soon we came to the head of a dirt road marked by an old, splintering wooden sign.

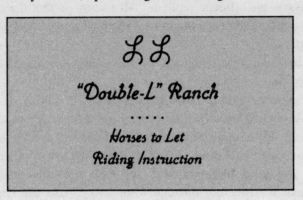

L L

"Double-L" Ranch

. . . . .

Horses to Let
Riding Instruction

"This must be it," I said.

Becca and I walked down the dirt road, passing a fenced-in corral with five horses standing inside it, their tails flicking.

I stopped for a moment to admire them. One in particular, a large white one with a thick mane, caught my eye. The horse snorted and stamped a bit as I gazed at him.

"Aren't they beautiful, Becca?" I sighed.

"They're cute," Becca agreed good-naturedly. She tugged on the sleeve of my pink tie-dyed shirt. "Come on, we'd better find the owners. What did Ranger Abe say their names were? The Flynns, that's it."

"That's strange," I said. "I wonder why it's called the Double-L Ranch if their name is Flynn."

"Maybe they're really bad spellers," Becca joked.

We continued up the dirt road until we came to a large

stable. In the distance was a quaint, white house with blue shutters. Looking at the house I thought about how strange it would be to live there, inside the park, like that. I noticed that both the stable and the house looked clean, but a little run-down, as if they could use a fresh coat of paint.

A banging sound, like hammering, came from inside the stable. Becca and I headed toward it.

It took a few moments for my eyes to adjust to the darkness inside the stable after the bright sunlight outside. As they did, I looked around. There were no horses, only empty stalls. Crouched in one corner, with his back to us, was a sandy-haired guy dressed in overalls and a white T-shirt.

"Excuse me," I said during a pause in his hammering. "Can you help us? We're looking for—"

But he paid no attention to me and just went on hammering.

Becca and I exchanged glances.

"Boy, talk about unfriendly," I muttered.

"*Excuse* me," Becca tried, louder than I had.

But he continued to ignore us. Then, all of a sudden, I realized why.

"He's wearing headphones," I said to Becca. I couldn't help laughing a little at the fact that I hadn't figured that out right away—especially considering that I probably use my own headphones more than anyone I know. *After all,* I reminded myself, *you're the one who always says that everything in life seems better with background music.*

I walked over to the guy and tapped him on the shoulder.

He spun to face me, his deep green eyes flashing with alarm. Then his face relaxed. He took off his headphones and let them hang around his neck.

"Wow, you really startled me," he said.

"Sorry," I replied.

"We tried calling out when we first came in, but you didn't hear us," Becca added.

"We don't get a lot of visitors around here." He grinned a little sheepishly and touched one hand to his headphones. "And I always listen to music when I work."

I nodded. "Believe me, I understand." Just then I noticed the strains of a familiar song playing tinnily out from his headphones. "Hey," I said, "is that 'Dreaming Green' by Pop Quiz?"

His eyes widened in surprise. "Yeah. You know it?"

"Sure," I said. "That's from their first CD. It's good, but the new one's even better."

"That's what I've heard," he replied. "I don't have it yet, though."

"I just got it last week," I told him.

"It's next on my list," he said with a grin.

"The new Hot Potatoes CD is really good, too," I told him.

"I know," he replied with enthusiasm. "I love the Hot Potatoes."

I almost couldn't believe my ears. This guy liked the exact same music I did!

"Excuse me, you guys," Becca said with a laugh, "but

34

before we continue with the countdown of the top ten alternative bands of the week—"

I laughed, too. "Oh, right. Sorry. I almost forgot why we were here."

"Do you want to rent a horse or something?" the guy asked, sounding hopeful.

"Oh, no," I answered quickly. "Nothing like that. I mean, I'd love to, but we're here looking for the Flynns."

"Do you know where they are?" Becca asked.

"Well, I'm a Flynn," he offered with a grin. "Matt Flynn."

I looked at him. *Didn't Ranger Abe say the Flynns were an older couple? This guy looks only a little bit older than me.*

"Is this *your* ranch?" I asked him doubtfully.

"It's my family's," Matt explained. "Actually, my grandparents run the place. But I'm here helping out right now. My grandfather broke his leg, and my grandmother can't take care of him and the ranch all by herself."

"That's terrible about your grandfather," Becca said.

Matt nodded. "He was thrown by a horse. It was the first bad accident he's had in fifty years of running the ranch."

"What happened?" I asked.

"He was riding up on one of the mountain ridges around here on a big white stallion named Blizzard. For some reason Blizzard got spooked and threw him," Matt explained.

"Is Blizzard that big white one we saw in the pen with the other horses on our way in?" I asked.

Matt nodded. "He can be pretty high-strung. Usually my

grandfather's the only one who can really handle him. But something must have happened that day. Anyway, what is it you want to see my grandparents about?"

"We want to know if they had a copy of the map of the park's horse trails," Becca responded.

"We work for the park," I explained. "We're junior rangers. Some of the old horse trails connect with some of the park's trails, and hikers have been getting confused. The park wants a copy of the trail map so we can mark the locations of the horse trails on the hiking trail map, too."

"I'm sure my grandparents have one," Matt replied. "I remember them from when I was little. Although I don't think anyone's asked for one of those in years."

"How come?" I asked. "I heard there used to be a lot of riding in the park. What happened?"

"A bunch of ranches closed, for one thing," Matt said. "I guess it all started with old man Slocum's place. It was over on a mountain just east of here. I remember he had a lot of horses back when I used to visit when I was a little boy. But then he died and he had no one to leave the place to. So he left it to the park."

"What happened then?" Becca asked.

"I think the park tried to run the place as a ranch for a while, but they really didn't know what they were doing," Matt explained. "They probably should have brought in someone who knew about horses. Anyway, eventually they ended up turning the place into a mountain biking area."

"You're kidding!" I said in amazement. I knew the area

he meant very well. "The mountain biking area used to be a horse ranch?"

Matt nodded. "Then, as stuff like biking and canoeing and whitewater rafting became more popular, fewer and fewer people wanted to tour the park on horseback. Soon the other ranches closed down, too." He shrugged. "All except us."

"That's so sad," Becca said.

"It's terrible!" I agreed. "I bet it must be incredible to see the park on horseback."

"Why don't you give it a try," Matt suggested with a grin. "We have a special rental rate for junior rangers, I'm sure."

"Sounds great, except I don't know how to ride," I said. "Actually, I wanted to take some lessons, but . . . well, my family doesn't really have a lot of extra money for stuff like that now."

Matt nodded reassuringly. "I know what you mean. Things aren't exactly easy for any of us here at the ranch right now, either. My grandparents are getting older. They should probably hire someone to help out here, but they can't afford it. They just don't have the business anymore."

"That's too bad," Becca said.

"Once in a while someone stops by to hire a horse, and a couple of kids from town come by for lessons," Matt explained. "But it's getting harder and harder for my grandparents to make ends meet." A worried expression crossed his face, and he paused, as if he were thinking about something. Then he shook his head and smiled again and looked at me earnestly. "But maybe we can work something out for you anyhow. You know, a way that you could get some lessons without having to pay for them."

"Oh, no, thanks anyway," I said quickly. "I definitely wouldn't feel right about that. It sounds like you already have enough to do around here without giving away free lessons."

"Sophie, maybe you could help out on the ranch in exchange for the lessons," Becca suggested.

"That's a great idea!" Matt agreed, his green eyes sparkling. "I mean, that is, if you want to."

"I'd love to," I said sincerely.

"Then it's a deal," Matt said with a grin. "You can have your first lesson tomorrow afternoon, if you want. You could come by about one, and I'll show you around the ranch first."

"I'll be here," I said happily. *This is great,* I thought. *By helping out on the ranch I'll get to spend lots of time getting to know the horses . . . and Matt.*

Suddenly Matt's expression darkened. His eyes seemed focused on something in the distance, something behind me.

I turned to look, but I didn't see anything. I turned back to him.

"Listen, I can't talk anymore right now," Matt said quickly. "I have to find my grandparents. You'd better go."

"Um, okay," I said, a little confused. *What just came over him?* I wondered. *His whole attitude suddenly seemed to change.*

"What about the horse trail map, Matt?" Becca reminded

him. "Maybe you should ask your grandparents about it before we—"

"I can't," Matt cut her off. "Not now. I really have to go."

Without another word he turned abruptly and hurried away from us, toward the white house in the distance.

Becca and I stared at each other in astonishment.

"What was that all about?" I wondered out loud.

"Maybe he saw a ghost or something," Becca joked. "Come on, we'd better go. Carson, Alex, and Kayla must be waiting for us on the trails. You can get the map when you come back tomorrow."

"I guess so," I said. But inside, I felt uneasy. In a way, it was almost as if Matt *had* seen a ghost.

Then, as Becca and I started back down the dirt road, I spotted something in the distance, on the mountain road to our right. It was a car, a big black shiny car. It was not the kind of car you usually saw in the park. And it was headed our way.

Moments later, the car turned on to the dirt road itself.

"Wow, look at that," Becca commented as the huge shiny car drove past us, with whoever was inside hidden by its dark frosted windows. "I guess Matt and his grandparents are expecting some pretty fancy visitors."

"I guess so," I echoed.

But as I turned to watch the car drive on toward the ranch, I still couldn't seem to shake the feeling of uneasiness that had come over me.

FOUR

Later that afternoon I wiped the sweat from my forehead for what seemed like the millionth time.

"Phew!" I sighed, taking a final smack at the head of the wooden stake with my mallet. "How many more of these things do we have to go?"

Alex walked over to me. "Here," she said, holding out the little pot of red paint in her hand. "You take another turn painting for a while. I can hammer the stakes."

"No, that's okay," I said. Alex and I had agreed to split the work. She'd drive half of the wooden stakes into the ground while I painted the markers, and then we'd switch. I wasn't about to go back on the deal now, no matter how sore my shoulders were getting.

Alex shrugged and squatted down in front of the stake to give it a dab of red paint. The two of us were finishing up replacing and repairing the markers on the red trail. Alex, Carson, and Kayla had already finished the blue trail by the time Becca and I had made our way back from the ranch. Now Carson, Kayla, and Becca were working on the green trail while Alex and I did the red.

The two of us continued along the trail, scanning it for missing markers. The red trail started in the woods and made its way around a low mountain ridge before returning to the reservoir area and meeting up with the other trails. Between the trees to my left I could see a valley below, as well as an occasional sparkle of reflected light from the river.

Soon the path curved to the right a bit, bringing us closer to the edge of the ridge. The trail marker there was in pretty good shape but faded in color, so Alex bent down to paint it. Meanwhile, I gazed out at the incredible view—the other mountains in the distance, the blue sky without a single cloud, and the river, which was in full sight now.

Suddenly, I spotted a familiar dark red building just a bit downstream of where we were standing.

"Hey, it's the mill!" I said, recognizing it at once.

Alex stood up and walked over beside me. "Oh, wow, a mill," she said, peering down toward the river. "And look at that great waterwheel." There was obvious admiration in her voice.

"You mean that big wheel with the paddles?" I asked. "What's that for, anyway?"

"That's what used to power the mill," Alex explained.

"There was usually some kind of waterway which came through a trough, or a sluice, from somewhere farther upstream. That water poured down onto the waterwheel like a waterfall, making the waterwheel turn. Then there were gears inside the building that were turned by the wheel, kind of like giant bicycle gears. All the machinery in the building operated that way. They didn't even need electricity."

I looked at her. Her big brown eyes were shining with excitement. Alex is really into machinery and cool inventions, and she's practically nuts about anything that involves wheels.

"I wonder what kind of mill it was, anyway," Alex said.

"What do you mean?" I asked.

"You know, what they made there," she said. "There are all kinds of mills: corn mills, wheat mills, pulp mills—"

"I think it was a paper mill," I said, remembering the sign.

Alex nodded. "A paper mill. That makes sense. I guess at one time a lot of the trees from these forests were cut down to make paper."

"Imagine what this place would be like with the trees cut down," I said.

"Yeah, I guess it's a good thing they decided to make the area into a park," Alex commented. "I wonder when that was, exactly."

"I guess we can always ask Ranger Abe next Saturday at the meeting," I suggested.

"Or just use a computer and look it up on the Internet," Alex pointed out.

Just then I spotted something out of the corner of my eye. It was a piece of garbage—a slip of paper—that had blown up against the trunk of a tree.

Remembering the way Kayla had cleaned the cans and wrappers out of the stream the other day, I walked over toward the paper.

"I think it's so inconsiderate when hikers leave their garbage on the trails," I commented, picking up this new bit of trash.

"Definitely," Alex agreed.

"Hmmm, land surveyors. I wonder what that's from," Alex said, looking over my shoulder.

"What *is* a land surveyor anyway?" I asked her.

"It's someone who makes notations of the relationships between certain measurements in an environment, like horizontal distances, elevations, and angles," she replied. "You know what I mean?"

"Not really," I admitted. When Alex starts talking technical stuff, I'm totally lost. Sometimes I wonder if *anyone* can understand her. I laughed. "Can you maybe explain it in English?"

She laughed, too. "Just think of it as someone who takes measurements of the landscape," she tried.

"Okay," I said. Then I thought of something. "But why would anyone want to measure the landscape, anyway?"

"Well, to make a map, for one thing," Alex replied.

"Oh," I said. I'd always sort of wondered how people were able to make maps.

"Surveyors are also used for construction projects," Alex

Sansevere Licensed Land Surveyors

serving Cayenga County since 1948

2357 Cove Drive, Cayenga, CA Tel# 555-3400

Client #: __198237__

Date: __November 7__

N86°0300 E
+387'

N85°1400" E
+387'

CAYENGA RIVER

went on. "You know, to sort of get the lay of the land before any building begins. A surveyor came to my family's house last year, before our new wing was built."

"New *wing*?" I repeated incredulously. I laughed. "What do you live in, an airplane?"

Alex laughed a little, too. But it was a funny laugh, almost an embarrassed-sounding laugh. And I noticed two bright pink spots on her pale cheeks.

"I guess my house *is* kind of big," she said softly, turning away from me. Then she stared up the trail ahead of me. "Come on, we'd better get going and finish these markers."

I stared after Alex in amazement. It didn't really surprise me to hear that Alex lived in a big house. I already knew she lived in Cayenga Heights, which is this really fancy area in the cliffs south of the park. And a couple of weeks earlier she had mentioned that she had a pool.

No, it didn't surprise me to think that Alex might be pretty rich. What did surprise me was the way she seemed to feel about it, almost like she was ashamed of it or something. *I'd never feel that way if I were rich,* I decided, stuffing the piece of paper in the pocket of my purple suede vest. *I'd be totally happy if my family could afford stuff like big houses in Cayenga Heights and swimming pools and riding lessons. Alex just doesn't know how good she really has it.*

"That's it, Sophie!" Matt called encouragingly. "Stay in control. Don't let the horse think she's in charge. Remember, you're the boss."

"Sure thing," I said, bouncing around in the saddle. "Just tell that to the horse, okay?"

It was Sunday afternoon, and I was having my first riding lesson with Matt. Before the lesson I had helped Matt clean out some stalls and groom a few of the horses. Now I was perched in the saddle on top of Rosemary, a gray and white dappled mare that Matt recommended as a nice gentle horse for me to start out with.

Rosemary had seemed gentle enough when I was on the ground feeding her a carrot before the lesson. But now that I was riding her around the paddock, she suddenly appeared to be about twice as big—and about twice as fast, too.

"Hey, slow down!" I cried as Rosemary trotted around a corner.

"Tell her what you want her to do in a way she can understand," Matt reminded me from his seat on the fence.

What's that supposed to mean? I thought in a panic. Then I remembered. I pulled back on the reins. Miraculously, Rosemary slowed to a walk.

I shot Matt a grin. "It worked!"

He smiled back at me. "I had a feeling it would. Now, ease up on the reins a little. Don't pull too hard. And don't grip too tight with your legs. Go easy."

"But I thought I was supposed to show her that I was the boss," I objected.

"You are," Matt said. "But you're also supposed to have a soft hand and stay relaxed."

I managed to bring the horse to a stop in front of where

Matt was sitting on the fence. "It's hard to do both things at once," I said.

Matt thought a moment. "Okay, then, try thinking of Alyssa Raith," he suggested. "Do you like her music?"

"Of course, I love it," I said. I laughed. "But how's that supposed to help my riding?"

"Think of the way Alyssa Raith sings and plays guitar," Matt said. "She sounds relaxed and soft, but she's also totally in control."

I grinned. Matt had just pointed out the very thing that I loved the most about Alyssa Raith's music.

"I know just what you mean," I said. "Okay, I'll give it a try."

Pressing gently into the horse's side with my right foot, I eased Rosemary back into her walk around the paddock. Then I began to hum my favorite Alyssa Raith song, "Free Spirit," under my breath. As the music filled my head I felt relaxed and confident. I guided Rosemary around the paddock, and I didn't even pull her back when she started to trot. I wasn't scared at all anymore. In fact, I was having a great time.

I circled the paddock on Rosemary a few more times and then brought her to a halt in front of Matt.

Matt's face was beaming. "That was great, Sophie. I think you might be ready to try one of the park trails next time."

"Really?" I said eagerly. "You mean it?"

"Sure," Matt said. He walked toward me and held Rosemary's reins while I dismounted. "You looked like a pro there."

"Thanks," I said with pride.

"Very nice riding indeed," said a voice just beyond the rail.

I turned and saw an older woman leaning on the fence looking at us, a smile on her tanned, wrinkled face. Her white hair was pulled into a soft bun, and she wore dark blue jeans and a pink and white checkered blouse with a brown leather vest. Even from there I could see that her eyes were the exact same color green as Matt's.

"Hi, Gran," Matt greeted her. "This is Sophie. She just had her first lesson. Sophie, this is my grandmother, Lulu Flynn."

"Nice to meet you, Mrs. Flynn," I said.

"Oh, call me Lulu," she replied with a wave of her hand. "I always think 'Mrs. Flynn' was a name that belonged to my mother-in-law." She chuckled. "So, Sophie, Matt tells me you're with the junior rangers."

"That's right," I answered.

"You must be part of that new girls' division I read about in the paper, then," Lulu Flynn said. "What is it they're calling them now, 'the Girl Command' or something?"

"GIRLS R.U.L.E.," I answered with a smile. "It stands for 'Girls' Ranger Unit Learning Extension.'"

"That's a great name," Matt said.

"Very clever," Lulu agreed. "I hear you girls are real local heroes. From what I read you rescued Mesa del Oro from quite an awful fate."

On our first junior ranger assignment, a survival camping

trip, Becca, Kayla, Carson, Alex, and I had managed to stop a forest fire on the park's highest mountain. The local paper, *The Cayenga Echo,* had written a story about us.

"Wow, you didn't tell me you were a hero, Sophie," Matt said.

"You didn't ask me," I replied with a grin.

He laughed. "Well, I'm impressed."

"Now if only there were some way to save *our* little part of the park from its fate," his grandmother said, a sad, faraway look coming to her eyes.

I glanced at Matt, but he didn't meet my gaze. Instead, he cleared his throat and quickly changed the subject. "So, Sophie, when should we schedule your next lesson? How about Tuesday afternoon? I could take you out on one of the trails."

"Okay, sure," I agreed.

"Well, we'd better go in and check on your grandpa," Lulu Flynn said in a tired-sounding voice. "He'll be wanting his supper in a little while, and he can't do a thing for himself until that leg is healed."

"Okay, Gran, sure," Matt said. He unhitched the paddock gate and we both stepped out. "See you Tuesday, Sophie."

"See you then, Matt," I replied. I turned to look at Rosemary, who was standing in a corner of the paddock, flicking her tail at some flies. "Bye, Rosemary!"

Matt and his grandmother turned and headed toward the house, and I made my way back down the dirt road. As I did, I wondered what it was his grandmother had meant about wishing her part of the park could be saved from its fate. *What fate?* I asked myself. *Maybe she was only talking about the ranching business and how bad it's gotten in the past years,* I thought. Still I wasn't sure.

As I got to the end of the dirt road, I had a realization. I had just scheduled a riding lesson for next Tuesday. But I had to work in the park on Tuesday! I turned to call to Matt, but he and Lulu were out of sight.

I headed briskly back up the dirt road, passing the paddock. There was no sign of Matt in the stable, so I started in the direction of the white house with the blue shutters.

As I approached the porch, I could hear voices coming through the screen door. I recognized Matt's voice, as well as his grandmother's. There was also a man's voice, which I assumed belonged to Matt's grandfather.

I raised my hand to knock on the frame of the screen door. As I did, I heard Matt's grandmother say "Oh, Lester, maybe we just have to learn to accept this after all."

I paused for a moment and listened.

"I can't agree with you there, Lulu," Matt's grandfather replied. "I don't have a good feeling about this whole thing. I'll tell you something else, too. I don't think we should have handed over those maps, either!"

My heart skipped a beat. *Maps?* I thought. *Could he be talking about the horse trail maps Becca and I asked for?* Matt had given me a couple earlier that day. In fact, at that moment they were neatly folded in the back pocket of my green vintage bell-bottoms.

I continued listening, frozen in place.

"I don't like it at all," his grandfather continued. "I don't like strangers—and I definitely don't think this is a good time to be letting one into our lives."

I felt my heart rise into my throat. *A stranger in their lives? Could that mean me?* I wondered.

"Oh, maybe you're right, Lester," Matt's grandmother said. "I can't talk any more about it now anyway. I've got to get this wet laundry out on the line."

"I'll help you, Gran," Matt volunteered.

I heard footsteps headed toward the door. Quickly, I ducked around the corner of the house.

The screen door opened with a squeak. I crouched in the shadows, waiting.

"I'm worried about your grandpa," Matt's grandmother said, her voice louder now. "He's taking everything so hard these days. And he just doesn't seem to realize that we can't carry on on our own like this forever."

I strained to hear Matt's response, but they were out of earshot.

My mind was racing. *Was it possible that they were talking about me? That Matt's grandfather was upset that Matt had agreed to give me lessons in exchange for helping out around the ranch? What was it his grandmother had said? That they couldn't carry on on their own forever. Well, I was here to help out however I could, but only if they wanted me.*

As I turned and hurried back down the dirt road toward

the river, I felt an ache in my throat. The ranch meant so much to me already. I'd been so excited about my lessons and about working with Matt and the horses. But how could I still feel good about it after what I'd just heard?

FIVE

That night, I lay in my bed, tossing and turning. It's always been really hard for me to sleep when I have something on my mind. This time I just couldn't seem to stop thinking about what I'd overheard at the Flynns' ranch that afternoon.

I sighed. Lemonade, my golden retriever, stood up from her spot on the rag rug by my bed and walked over to me. She poked her cold nose into my arm.

I rolled over to face her. "Hi, girl."

Lemonade started panting. I could feel her hot breath on my arm.

"What do you think, Lem?" I asked her. "Were they talking about me?" I scratched her behind the ears.

Lemonade let out a little whimper.

"I know, girl, I know," I said to her. "It's hard for me to

figure out, too. In one way it sounds silly, right? Why would Matt's grandfather be so against having me help out on the ranch? I mean, they *need* help, right?"

Lemonade wagged her tail.

"But on the other hand," I went on, "who *else* could they have been talking about? Matt said himself that nobody's asked his grandparents for any of those old maps in a long time. It had to be about me, right?"

Lemonade whined.

I moved over on the bed. "Oh, all right, girl," I said, tapping the mattress. "Come on up."

Lemonade jumped onto the bed, shaking the mattress.

"Ooof," I said as one of her paws landed smack in the middle of my stomach. "You're not exactly a puppy anymore, Lem. I'm not sure there's room up here for both of us."

I scooted over and managed to wriggle into an almost comfortable position, wedged against the wall. Lemonade put her head down on my stomach with a sigh.

"Well, Lem, there's only one way to find out for sure," I said. I stroked her head. "I'm just going to have to go and confront Matt about it myself. I mean, I'm just not the kind of person who can stand to sit back and guess about stuff like this. If Matt or his family has a problem with my working on the ranch, I should just go there and hear it for myself, face-to-face. Right, Lem?"

Lemonade was still.

"Lem?"

The only reply was a long, loud dog snore. I gave

Lemonade one more scratch on the head and then drifted off to sleep myself.

The following morning, I stood in front of the refrigerator, fingering the strap of my faded overalls and looking for the orange juice.

A moment later, my mom came into the room, dressed in her work uniform.

"Sophie, don't just stand there with the door open," she said. "You're driving up the electric bill. And you're wasting energy, too," she added. She began fumbling in her uniform pockets. "Now, where did I put those car keys?"

"I'm just looking for the OJ," I explained.

"Your brother must have finished it," she replied. "There's another can in the freezer you can make up if you want." She dumped out a little container of keys, coins, and other small items on the counter. "I can't understand it. I had them in my hand when I came in last night."

I closed the refrigerator door and opened the freezer.

"Here they are!" my mother said triumphantly behind me. "Oh, wait, Soph, I forgot! Don't make up that juice after all. Not until I get some bottled water."

"Bottled water?" I repeated in surprise. My mother definitely wasn't the type to buy bottled water. And definitely not to mix up the orange juice with.

"The Health Department has declared a Water Alert for all of Cayenga County," my mother explained. "It was all over the radio this morning. One of the county reservoirs failed a safe drinking water test."

"Which reservoir?" I asked, spinning to face her. "Was it the one in the park?"

"Yes, I think they said it was," my mother responded. "They found traces of some kind of chemical."

I stared at her. "Did you say a chemical?"

My mother nodded. "I think they might have said it was chlorine. But I'm not sure. Anyway, there was enough of it to declare a Water Alert. They said on the news that an Alert isn't as serious as a Warning. They don't tell you not to drink it unless it's an actual Warning. But I think we'd better stay on the safe side until they get the problem cleared up."

"Definitely," I agreed. There was something very weird going on with the reservoir water. *I wonder what—or who—could be responsible for this,* I thought.

"Well, I'm not drinking it," Becca announced later that day.

"My mom said she thinks it's safer not to," I agreed, twisting open the top on my bottle of apple juice.

"You'd better watch out for that soda then, Becca," warned my friend Miranda Ruiz. "I think they mix it up here at the cafeteria, and they probably use tap water in the soda fountain."

"Yech!" Becca exclaimed, pushing the paper cup on the table away from her.

It was lunchtime, and the three of us were sitting in the cafeteria together, eating lunch and talking about the Health Department's Water Alert.

"Hey, there's Carson," I said, spotting Carson across the room with a tray of food in her hands. I waved to get her attention.

After a moment, Carson caught my eye.

Come sit with us, I mouthed.

Carson nodded.

I shook my head in amazement. I think it is so cool the way Carson can read lips. I'd never be able to tell what someone was mouthing silently to *me* from across the room like that.

Carson made her way toward us and sat down opposite Miranda and me, next to Becca.

"Hi," she said cheerfully. "Hey, do you guys know about the Water Alert?"

I nodded. "At the park reservoir. We were just talking about it before you came over. What do you think it's all about?"

"I don't know," Carson replied gravely. "First there was that problem last week, and now this. Whatever it is, it's getting worse. My mom said there's never been anything like this in the park before. At least, not as long as she's been a ranger. She talked to Ranger Abe this morning, but he doesn't know any more about it."

"It was some kind of chemical they found, right?" Miranda asked. "That's what they said on *Good Morning Southern California* this morning."

Carson nodded. "I think it was chlorine."

"Chlorine? Maybe someone was trying to turn the reservoir into a swimming pool," Becca joked.

"That garbage Kayla and I found the other day was in one of the streams that feeds into the reservoir," I volunteered. "But Alex said she didn't think that would have anything to do with it."

"Actually, don't they put chlorine into our drinking water anyway?" Miranda asked. "I thought I heard that once."

"Alex would know all about this stuff," I said.

"Good point, Sophie," Carson agreed. "Let's ask her what she thinks tomorrow when we see her at the park."

"Hey, speaking of the park, how are your riding lessons going, Sophie?" Becca asked.

"Not so great," I answered glumly.

"What do you mean?" Carson asked.

"Yeah, I thought you were really looking forward to those lessons, Sophie," Miranda said, her voice filled with concern. "What happened?"

Quickly, I explained what had happened after my lesson the day before, how I had walked back to the house and overheard Matt and his grandparents talking.

"Oh, Sophie, they probably didn't mean you at all," Miranda said when I had finished.

"No way," Becca agreed. "I mean, I've never met Matt's grandparents, but I can tell you for sure that Matt, for one, definitely likes having you around the ranch." Her green eyes twinkled mischievously. "I could see it the first day you two were together."

I smiled. *So Becca noticed how well Matt and I got along, too,* I thought happily.

"That conversation you overheard must have been about something completely different," Miranda said reassuringly.

"But like what?" I said a little skeptically. "Matt's grandfather was talking about someone who had asked for maps. That couldn't have been anyone else." I turned to Becca.

60

"Remember? Matt told us that no one had asked for one of those old horse trail maps in ages."

"I guess you do have a point," Becca admitted.

"And they were also talking about letting a stranger into their lives," I reminded them. "That had to mean me. Matt told us that his grandparents don't even get many visitors out there, right?"

"That's true," Becca murmured. Then her face lit up. "Hey, Sophie, what about that car we saw as we were leaving that day? Maybe those were the strangers Matt and his grandparents were talking about!"

"Oh my gosh, you're right!" I said. "I forgot all about that. As Becca and I were leaving on Saturday we saw a big fancy car drive up to the ranch," I explained to the others. "We figured it must be someone visiting the Flynns." Then I thought of something. "Becca, that could even be why Matt was acting so funny all of a sudden! You know, why he ran back to the house like that. Maybe he saw the car coming around the mountain before we did."

"But who could have been in the car?" Carson wondered.

"Beats me," I said.

"Someone Matt wasn't too happy about seeing, I'd say," Becca said.

Becca has a good point, I realized. *Maybe Matt and his family were talking about whoever had been in that car, after all. Maybe it wasn't about me at all.*

Either way, I decided, *I've got a lot to ask Matt about. I'm going to head over to the ranch right after school and try to get this whole thing straightened out for good.*

61

SIX

"Whoa! Whoa, boy!"

I could hear Matt's voice echoing from the paddock as I made my way up the dirt road toward the ranch later that afternoon. As I rounded the bend, I was surprised to see that Matt was riding Blizzard, the large white stallion I had seen on my first visit to the ranch.

"I thought you said your grandfather was the only person who could handle Blizzard," I said, leaning against the paddock fence.

Matt looked up, startled. "Sophie, hi," he said. Blizzard started to shake and buck underneath him. "Whoa, hold on there, boy!"

I watched as Matt managed to bring the horse under control. He trotted Blizzard to a corner of the paddock and dismounted, looping the horse's reins around a fence post.

Matt walked over to me. "My grandfather *is* the only one who can really handle Blizzard, believe me," he said, brushing the dust off his jeans. "I've been thrown twice this afternoon."

"Then why are you riding him?" I asked, puzzled. "I mean, why not choose a gentler horse?"

"The longer Blizzard goes without a rider, the wilder he'll become," Matt explained. "I can't let him get used to not being ridden, or he'll be no good for anyone to ride, ever. And, since my grandfather can't ride him until his leg's better, it's up to me." Matt grinned. "Unless you'd like to give him a try."

"Thanks anyway," I said, "but I'll stick to Rosemary." Then I remembered why I had come, what I wanted to talk to Matt about. I studied his face for a moment, trying to think of how to say what I wanted to.

Matt gazed back at me. His eyes were at first questioning, and then filled with concern. "What is it, Sophie?" he asked me gently. "What's the matter?"

"I need to ask you about something," I began.

"Sure, go ahead," Matt urged.

"It's something that happened yesterday, after our lesson," I said. "After I said good-bye to you I realized I couldn't make it to another lesson on Tuesday. I have to work in the park that day."

"Is that all you're worried about, Sophie?" Matt's face relaxed with relief. "I thought it was something much more serious. Sure, we can change the lesson to anytime you want."

"No, that's not it, Matt," I said. "There is something more. Like I said, I realized I couldn't make it to the lesson. So I turned back to find you. You weren't around anywhere, and I figured you'd gone into the house, so I went that way, too."

Matt looked confused. "You came to the house on Sunday? But I didn't see you."

"That's because I stayed outside the door. You see, I heard something," I explained a little sheepishly. "I didn't mean to eavesdrop. I was about to knock on the door . . ." I stopped, a little embarrassed to admit I'd been listening in on his family's conversation.

"Don't worry about it," Matt said. "Just go on. Tell me. Tell me what you heard."

"It was your grandfather," I explained. "At least, it must have been him. He was talking about handing over some maps—and about a stranger in your lives."

Matt's face darkened. "Oh. So, you heard all that," he said in a low voice. "So I guess now you know."

Then it was true! I couldn't believe it! I didn't know what to say.

"Matt," I said finally, my throat feeling tight, "why didn't you just tell me?"

Matt sighed. "I guess I should have, Sophie. But I just didn't want to burden you with our family problems."

"Even if those family problems happen to be about *me*?" I said incredulously.

Matt stared at me. "Sophie, what are you talking about?"

"The same thing you're talking about," I said. "That your

grandfather doesn't want me taking lessons or helping out on the ranch!"

Matt's mouth dropped open.

"Isn't that what you're talking about?" I asked uncertainly.

"No, of course not!" Matt replied. "Where did you get that idea?"

"From just what I told you," I said. "I heard your grandfather talking."

Matt shook his head and laughed a little. "Sophie, I don't know what you heard, or what you *think* you heard, but believe me, you got it all wrong."

"I did?" I asked.

"As wrong as can be," Matt assured me. He looked at me and smiled. "Come on, let's go saddle up Rosemary and another horse and go for a ride on the trails. I'll tell you all about what's really going on while we're out there."

Fifteen minutes later, Matt and I were riding through the woods just outside the Flynns' property. The sun was shining through the bright green leaves above us, and birds were twittering in the trees. The trail was just wide enough for two riders, and Rosemary ambled along, shoulder to shoulder with Chocolate, Matt's chestnut mare.

At first, Matt was silent. I was tempted to ask him a million questions. I was dying to find out exactly what was going on, to know what it was his grandfather had been talking about. But something told me to wait. *I have a feeling this isn't going to be easy for Matt to talk about, whatever it is,* I thought. *It's not fair to ask him to start before he's ready.*

After a few moments, Matt began to speak. "Sophie, this ranch has been in my family for generations. In fact, there have been Flynns in this part of California since the Gold Rush." He laughed. "Actually, since just after the Gold Rush. According to family legend, my great-great-great-uncle Floyd Flynn got here just a little too late, after pretty much all of the gold had already been claimed."

I laughed, too. "Sounds like me," I said. "I never make it anywhere on time."

"You were on time for your lesson yesterday," Matt pointed out.

I hadn't even realized that. "I guess that was important to me," I said softly. "Anyway, go on. You were telling me about the Flynns."

"What I'm trying to say is that the Flynns have been through a lot here," Matt continued. "The Flynn ranch was around way before the park was even here. Back then it was called the Good Luck Ranch. Then, when my grandpa and grandma met and got married, they changed the name to the Double-L, for their names, Lulu and Lester." He grinned. "They said finding each other was all the luck either one of them ever needed."

"That's so sweet," I said.

"My great-grandparents owned the place back when the park was first created in the 1930s," Matt went on. "Since the parklands were going to extend around the ranch on all sides, there was a special allowance made for our family and for a few others who already owned land here so we could keep our property. The rest of the land was given over to the Parks Department."

"I get it," I said. "You mean the only people who are allowed to own land inside the park are people who already owned it before the park was created?"

"Right," Matt said. "Unless we decide to sell it, of course. And that's where the problem comes in."

"What do you mean?" I asked.

"The stranger my grandfather was talking about is a man named Mr. Cramson," Matt went on. "He wants to buy the ranch from my grandparents."

"But the ranch has been in your family for generations, you just said so," I replied. "They're not going to sell it to him, are they?"

"They don't want to," Matt replied. "But my grandmother is starting to feel like they might have no choice. They can't go on working the place alone, and I can't be here to help them out all the time."

"I'll help anytime I can," I volunteered.

"I know, Sophie, and I appreciate it," Matt said. "We all do, believe me. But you can't be at the ranch all the time, either. My grandparents would need at least one full-time ranch hand to keep the place going. But there's no way they can afford that. Business is terrible. Nobody's interested in renting horses for the park anymore. And my grandparents are getting older. It might be time for them to just give it up."

Suddenly the trail came out of the woods beside a stream.

The horses headed straight for the water and began to drink.

I shook my head. "I still think they should do whatever they can to keep the ranch," I said stubbornly. I looked down at Rosemary, at her smooth gray coat. I fingered her silky mane as she drank. *What will happen to Rosemary and the other horses if the Flynns sell the ranch?* I wondered.

Matt sighed. "Believe me Sophie, I feel just as upset about it as you do. This ranch was supposed to be passed down to me one day. I've been dreaming about that ever since I was a little kid."

I looked at Matt. He seemed so sad.

"There has to be some way," I said with determination. "Something we can do."

"My grandparents don't want to see it go, either," Matt said. "The first time Mr. Cramson came and offered to buy the place, they just laughed. But then a few days later my grandfather broke his leg, and my grandmother started to think about it again. Mr. Cramson kept visiting, and I guess she started to get worn down. The last time he came, on Saturday, my grandmother told him she'd think about it."

"Was that his car I saw drive up to your place on Saturday when I left?" I asked Matt.

He nodded. "He asked for some maps of the trails, the same ones you wanted. My grandfather got so angry when he heard my grandmother had handed them over. He said it was as if Mr. Cramson thought he already owned the ranch, and all the horse trails, too. It didn't make sense. I mean, it was just a couple of maps. But I guess Grandpa was just worried he'd lose the ranch."

"What does this Mr. Cramdon guy want to do with the ranch?" I asked.

"Cramson," Matt corrected me. "I'm not sure. He says he might want to try to keep it going as a horse ranch, but I don't see how he can do it. It'll never survive, not with business the way it is. It'll probably just end up like old man Slocum's, made into a bike rental place or something else."

"Matt, we can't let this happen!" I insisted.

"I know, Sophie," Matt said sadly. "But what are we going to do?"

"I don't know yet," I said. "But we have to come up with something. The Double-L Ranch is the only working horse ranch left in the park! We can't just let it close!"

SEVEN

The following afternoon, I walked into the Park Headquarters building and over to the junior ranger schedule board to check the updated assignments. On Saturday Ranger Abe had told me to work the welcome booth at the campground this afternoon, but sometimes our assignments are changed at the last minute. That's one reason all the junior rangers check the board and sign in before heading to their posts.

Carson and Becca were already at the board when I got there.

"Hi, Sophie," Becca sang out.

"Hi," Carson said with a wave.

"Hi, you guys," I greeted them.

I was glad to see them, especially since I hadn't had a chance to talk to them in school that day. I really wanted to tell them all about the Double-L Ranch and Mr. Cramson, and to see if they had any ideas about how we could help the Flynns.

Still, I realized, *it probably makes more sense to wait until Alex and Kayla get here, too. That way I won't have to tell the story twice.* Even so, I felt like I was about to burst with the news.

"We were just talking about the Water Alert," Carson explained to me. "I heard from my mom that the Health Department lifted it today. They took another sample of the water at the reservoir this afternoon and it came up fine."

"That's good," I said. I could tell my mom was starting to get really stressed out about having to buy all that bottled water.

"I still feel creepy about drinking it," Becca said. "I mean, where did those chemicals, or chlorine, or whatever it was come from, anyway?"

"Here comes Alex," Carson said. "Let's ask her what she thinks."

Alex came walking toward us with Kayla at her side.

"Ask me what I think about what?" Alex wanted to know.

"The Water Alert," I said. "We heard it was chlorine they found. But my friend Miranda said that they put chlorine in our drinking water anyway. So which is it? Is chlorine bad, or good?"

"It's good in some ways and bad in others," Alex explained. "It's true that some chlorine goes into the water we drink. It helps kill germs that might be growing there. But it's only a little bit of chlorine, and it's supposed to happen once the water *leaves* the reservoir and goes down to the water filtration plant."

"So finding chlorine in the reservoir itself is weird because the water hasn't even been treated yet," Becca said. "Is that right?"

Alex nodded. "It also matters how much chlorine it was, and where they think it came from. Chlorine can produce dioxins, which are highly reactive compounds that can act like poisons—and even cause cancer. If those dioxins show up in the streams that feed into the reservoir, they can settle in the fish."

"Wow," Kayla said. "Can the fish die from that?"

"Sometimes," Alex told her. "The poisons also get into any wildlife that eat the fish—including humans. It can mess up the whole food chain."

"Yuck!" Becca said. "I'd hate to think that my stepfather might be serving poached fillet of dioxin down at the restaurant." She managed a laugh. "That could be really bad for business."

"Hey, you guys," I said, changing the subject, "speaking of bad business, I've got some pretty terrible news about the Double-L."

"What happened? Did you go talk to Matt yesterday?" Carson asked with interest. "Did you straighten everything out?"

"Kind of," I replied. "I mean, everything's okay between us, but it looks like the ranch might be in real danger."

"What do you mean?" Kayla asked, sounding worried. "What kind of danger?"

As quickly as I could I explained it all to them—about Mr. Cramson, and Matt's grandparents, and everything.

"That's really sad," Becca said when I'd finished. "The Flynns shouldn't have to sell the ranch if they don't want to."

"I know," I agreed. "Ranching is their whole way of life. It would be awful if they had to give it up."

"Did you say this Mr. Cramson wants to continue using it as a horse ranch?" Carson asked doubtfully. "Doesn't he know the business is failing? If the ranch can't survive with the Flynns running it, what makes him think it can survive when it's his?"

I shrugged. "Matt seems to think Mr. Cramson will try it for a while and then realize that same thing. Matt says Mr. Cramson will probably end up closing the place eventually and turning it into something else."

"Think of the poor horses," Kayla put in. "What will happen to them if the ranch closes?"

I shook my head. I didn't even like to think about that.

"It may not have to close after all. You know, it wouldn't be completely impossible for Mr. Cramson to make the horse ranch successful again," Alex said thoughtfully.

"What do you mean?" I asked.

"I'm just saying if he did some advertising he might be able to build the business up again," Alex said. "I'll bet one of the reasons no one wants to rent horses from the Flynns is that hardly anyone knows they're there."

"Hey, that's a great idea!" I said.

Kayla stared at me. "Sophie? Are you crazy? You mean to

74

say you'd actually *like* it if Mr. Cramson bought the ranch?"

"No, no," I said quickly. "I mean what Alex said before, about advertising. Don't you see? Why not do some advertising for the ranch right away, and build up the business now, while the Flynns still own it."

"Sophie, I hate to be the one to point this out, but you need *money* for advertising," Kayla said.

"Kayla's right," Becca agreed. "When my mom and my stepdad first opened their restaurant here a couple of months ago, they had to spend a lot on magazine ads and billboards and stuff. It's finally starting to pay off now because business is picking up for them, but it cost them a lot in the beginning."

"From what you've told us, Sophie, it definitely doesn't seem as if the Flynns have money for stuff like that," Carson said.

"Don't you see, they don't need money, though," I said excitedly. "The Flynns have the best park advertisers possible right here—*us!*"

"I get it," Kayla said, nodding. "Sophie's saying that we should start telling park visitors about the ranch."

"Exactly," I said. "Think about it. We see tons of people here in the park all the time. All we have to do is mention to them that there's another exciting park attraction that they may not know about—trail riding."

"Sure," Becca agreed. "That's called word-of-mouth advertising. My parents say that's the best kind there is—probably because it *can't* be bought."

"This could definitely work," Alex said. She began

calculating. "Let's see, there are five of us, and we're here three times a week. Each of us must speak to at least five to ten visitors each time we work, more if we're working one of the welcome booths—"

"Like I am today," I said, cutting her off and pointing to the schedule. "I'm stationed at the campground welcome booth this afternoon. That means I'll see every single camper who goes in or out. I'm definitely going to tell them all about the Double-L."

"I'm lifeguarding at the cove with Becca," Carson volunteered. "We'll try to tell people about it, too."

"I have another idea," Kayla said. "Didn't Ranger Abe say he was going to have new trail maps printed up soon?"

"That's right," Becca said. "He said he was planning to put some marks where the hiking trails meet up with the horse trails so that people won't get confused."

"Well, maybe we can persuade him to put more than just marks," Kayla suggested. "Maybe the new maps could show all of the horse trails as well as the hiking trails."

"That's a great idea," I agreed. "If people checking the trail maps see that there are horse trails, too, maybe they'll want to try out the riding."

"Let's definitely talk to him about it next time we see him," Kayla decided. "Meanwhile, we'll all try to carry out Sophie's plan as much as we can."

"Sure thing," Alex agreed.

Becca stood at attention and gave a mock salute. "The loyal troops of GIRLS R.U.L.E. are ready to begin Operation Word-of-Mouth, Sergeant Sophie."

We all laughed. I looked around at the smiling, eager faces of the four girls around me. I thought about how happy I was that they were going to try to help me save the Double-L. *I've got the greatest friends in the world,* I thought proudly. *If anyone can do it, we can.*

"Your campsite is number A37," I said, handing over a pamphlet and a receipt to the man standing with his little boy outside my booth. "Please remember to use the trash cans, not to feed the wildlife, and to put out your campfires when you're done. Enjoy your visit to the park."

"Thank you very much," the man replied, taking his receipt.

The little boy tugged on his father's hand. "Can I help you set up the tent, Daddy?"

"Of course, Nathan," the man replied. "Let me just ask this nice girl a question, and then we'll find our campsite." He turned to me again. "Is it all right to drink the water in the park now? We heard there was a problem."

"Yes, it's fine now," I assured him. "The water tested okay today."

"Good," the man replied. "Thank you." He turned to go.

"Oh, excuse me, sir?" I said.

He stopped. "Yes?"

"I just thought you might like to know that in addition to camping and the other activities in the park, there's a ranch that's offering horseback riding," I told him.

He raised his eyebrows. "Really? There's horseback riding here in the park? I didn't know that."

"Sure," I said eagerly. "In fact, you can even rent horses to take out on the trails. It's a really nice way to see the park."

"Daddy, I want to ride on a horse!" the little boy cried. "Can we, Daddy? Please?"

"Hold on a minute, Nathan," the man said. He turned back to me. "Just where is this place?"

"Not too far from here," I assured him. "It's in the Mill Valley section of the park. I can give you directions if you like. It's pretty easy."

"Can we please ride a horse, Daddy?" the little boy begged again.

His father smiled. "Yes, Nathan, we can ride a horse. I'll tell you what, we'll head over to this ranch first thing tomorrow, okay?"

"Yay!" Nathan cried happily. He threw his arms around his father's legs. "Daddy, this is going to be the bestest vacation ever!"

The father smiled at me. "I guess you'd better give me those directions."

"My pleasure," I said sincerely.

EIGHT

The following day, I stood in front of my locker at school, trying to find my math book hidden somewhere in the mess of books, papers, clothes, and other stuff.

The trick is to try to locate the book without starting an avalanche, I told myself as I pawed through my things.

Suddenly I heard Becca's voice behind me. "I wouldn't let the Health Department see this if I were you, Sophie. They might declare a 'locker alert.'"

"Very funny," I said, turning around. I sighed. "I can't seem to find my math book anywhere!"

"Isn't that it?" Becca asked, pointing.

I looked down at the ground. My green army surplus backpack with the hand-painted purple flowers was lying on its side on the floor in front of my locker. The top of the backpack was open, and my red math book was sliding out of it.

"Great, thanks," I said, scooping up the backpack and hoisting it onto my shoulder.

"What are you doing now, Sophie?" Becca asked. "Do you want to ride over to the park with me?"

"Okay, sure," I replied. Then I remembered something. "Becca, today's Wednesday. We don't work in the park on Wednesdays, do we?"

"No," Becca replied. "But my stepfather asked me to pick something up for him. There's this beekeeper in Mill Valley that makes some special kind of Cayenga Blossom Honey. Barry wants to make a honey-glazed duck dish for the special tomorrow at the restaurant. He asked me to pick up a few jars of this stuff for him."

"Sure, I'll go with you," I told her. It was a beautiful day out, perfect for a ride to the park. "But I don't have my bike. We'll have to stop by my place first."

Half an hour later, Becca and I rode our bikes down the mountain road that led toward Mill Valley. I had never approached the valley from this route, and it took a moment for me to recognize where I was. Soon I saw the roof of the old mill by the river, and shortly after that I recognized the Flynns' stable and house in the distance.

This is the same mountain road Mr. Cramson's car must have come down that day when Becca and I first went to the Double-L, I realized. I felt a pang. Just thinking about how the Flynns might lose their ranch made me feel awful.

"I think it's this way," Becca said, veering off the main road onto a smaller one.

I followed her on my bike, and together we descended into the lowest part of the valley.

Soon the small road turned into a dirt road that was very similar to the one that led to the ranch. I bumped along on my bike beside Becca, taking care to avoid the occasional sharp stones in the road.

After a few moments, we stopped our bikes in front of a gate with a small, hand-painted wooden sign.

"I guess this is it," Becca said, climbing off her bike.

"*The Busy Bee*"

APIARY

Delicious Cayenga Blossom Honey
Sold Here

We leaned our bikes against the fence and opened the gate. Inside, we followed the dirt path to a small wooden house that was painted a pretty shade of purple. Outside the house, flying from a small flagpole, was a wind sock that looked like a bumblebee.

We stepped up on the porch and Becca knocked on the door. After a few moments, we heard footsteps inside.

The door was answered by a young woman with two long blonde braids.

"Hi," the woman said with a friendly smile. "What can I help you with today?"

"I came to pick up some honey," Becca explained. "It's for the Cayenga Grill. I think my stepfather probably called you about it."

"Oh sure," the woman replied. "For Barry, right? I'm Stephanie. I've got the honey right back here. Come on in."

I followed Becca through the door and into the house. A man with a dark brown beard, his long hair pulled into a ponytail, sat on a rug in the living room, playing with a baby.

"Hi," he said to us cheerfully. He turned to the baby. "Say 'hi,' Blossom."

The baby cooed.

"I'll get your order," Stephanie said. "It's in the back room."

"Blossom—that's a cute name," I said. I squatted down to see the baby.

"I just hope it doesn't confuse the bees," Becca joked.

The man laughed. "I don't think that'll be a problem in the future," he said. "Stephanie and Blossom and I are probably moving to San Francisco soon." He turned to the baby. "You won't be seeing too many bees in the city, will you, Blossom?"

Blossom grabbed hold of his beard and smiled.

"My stepfather isn't going to like hearing that," Becca said. "He says your honey is the best he's ever tasted."

"Oh, he'll probably still be able to get it," the man said. "The new owner said he plans to continue running the place as an apiary."

"That's a fancy name for 'bee farm,' not an ape farm, by the way," said Stephanie, who had just come back into the room with several jars of honey in her arms. "Anyway, I promised I'd leave all the seeds and the honey specifications for Mr. Cramson when he takes over."

Becca and I looked at each other quickly.

"Did you say *Mr. Cramson* is going to buy this place?" I asked incredulously.

"That's right," Stephanie answered. "Why? Do you know him?"

"Not exactly," Becca replied.

"But we definitely know *about* him," I added. "Did you realize that Mr. Cramson wants to buy the horse ranch right next door to this?"

"No," Stephanie answered, looking surprised. She turned to the man. "Did you hear anything about that, Will?"

The man shook his head. "You mean the Double-L? I thought Cramson planned to make honey. I wonder what he wants with a ranch."

"Good question," Becca said.

"Mr. Cramson told the Flynns, the owners of the Double-L,

that he wants to keep on running their place as a horse ranch," I said.

"He sure is going to have his hands full if he wants to keep up this place, too," Will remarked.

"Maybe he's going to combine the two," Stephanie said. "You know, sort of make it into one big farm."

That made me think of something. "Are there any other people who own land inside the park near here?"

Stephanie nodded. "There's the Mill Valley Vineyard, just behind us. Two brothers run the place, I think. I can't remember their names just now. I think their land borders on the ranch and our place, though."

"Have you heard anything from these brothers about Mr. Cramson's trying to buy their land?" I asked.

Stephanie shook her head. "No, but we don't really see much of them, anyway."

"We don't see much of *anyone*," Will commented. "That's the main reason we're thinking of moving."

"When we first bought the place two years ago, we thought we'd love living here," Stephanie explained. "And it *is* beautiful. But we've got a lot of land, and so do our neighbors, so we're all pretty far apart. This isn't exactly a busy part of the park."

Will gazed at the baby. "We'd probably stay if it were just Stephanie and me. But we don't think it's good for Blossom to grow up in such an isolated place."

"Maybe if the honey business were doing a little better," Stephanie said dreamily. "Maybe then we could stay."

"If business picked up and there were lots of people

coming by, it probably wouldn't seem so lonely," Will agreed, bouncing Blossom on his knee.

Stephanie shrugged. "Anyway," she said, handing the jars over to Becca and me, "I hope you enjoy your honey."

"Yeah, stop by anytime," Will added. "Say 'bye-bye,' Blossom."

The baby cooed.

"Bye-bye," I said, waving to her. I nudged Becca when we got outside. "Did you hear all that?"

"I sure did," Becca said as we loaded the honey jars into her bike basket. "I wonder what's up."

"I do, too," I said. "We need more information. And I have a feeling I know where we can get it."

"Let me guess," Becca said with a smirk. "The Mill Valley Vineyard."

I nodded. "Come on," I said, straddling my bike. "Let's go."

Late the following afternoon, Becca, Carson, Kayla, Alex, and I sat around our favorite window table at the Cayenga Grill, Becca's family's restaurant. We had just finished up our shifts at the park, and we'd all agreed to meet at the restaurant to talk things over.

"Okay, let's look at this thing logically," Alex was saying, her serious brown eyes focusing on each one of us in turn. "What are the chances that this Mr. Cramson guy, whoever he is, actually wants to keep running the Double-L Ranch, the Busy Bee Apiary, and Mill Valley Vineyard?"

"I don't buy it at all," Kayla replied, popping a veggie nacho into her mouth.

"You don't have to," Becca snickered. "*Mr. Cramson*'s the one who wants to buy it—every bit of it he can, from what we can tell."

"I'm with Kayla on this," I said. "I definitely don't believe Mr. Cramson really wants to take over these three businesses. After all, none of them is doing very well at all."

"That's true," Alex agreed, serving herself some more french fried yams. "Sophie, from what you say, the Double-L is practically going out of business on its own."

"That's right," I told her. "And Stephanie and Will say their honey business isn't exactly busy, either."

"The Consuelo brothers, who run the vineyard, told us things are pretty slow for them, too," Becca reported. "In fact, they were really shocked when Mr. Cramson showed up asking to buy their land."

"Are they going to sell it to him?" Carson asked.

"They haven't decided," I replied. "One of them is convinced now that there must be gold or something under it. Otherwise why would Mr. Cramson want to buy it?"

"It's definitely not for gold," Alex said thoughtfully. "Gold has never been a very plentiful natural resource of the Cayenga County area."

"Too bad no one ever told Floyd Flynn that," I said, reaching for the platter of sesame noodles.

"Who?" Carson asked.

"An ancestor of Matt's," I explained. "He came out to this area to find gold during the Gold Rush times, but by the time he got here whatever little bit there was had all been claimed. That's why he started ranching."

"Wow," Becca commented. "Imagine, that ranch has been in the Flynn family since way back then."

"It seems so sad that they might have to give it up now," Kayla commented.

"Not if I can help it," I said with determination.

"There must be something else," Alex said, still looking thoughtful.

"Something else? What do you mean?" Carson asked. "Something else we can do?"

"I mean some other reason Mr. Cramson wants all that land," Alex replied.

"That is, assuming we're right, and he doesn't have a burning desire to run a ranch, an apiary, *and* a vineyard all at the same time," Becca reminded her.

"But what could it be?" Carson asked.

Alex shrugged. She paused and took a felt-tip pen out of the pocket of her red and purple striped T-shirt. "Anything, really. It might be that the land is rich in some other mineral, like iron ore, or it might be that there's natural gas there, or limestone." She picked up her napkin.

"That's a good idea," I urged. "Let's make a list of possibilities."

"But not on that napkin, Alex!" Becca objected. "It's cloth!"

"Ooops," Alex said, putting the napkin down with a sheepish expression. "Does anyone have a piece of paper?"

Sansevere Licensed Land Surveyors

serving Cayenga County since 1948

2357 Cove Drive, Cayenga, CA Tel# 555-3400

Client #:___198237___

Date:_November 7___

"Maybe I can get one from one of the waiters," Becca volunteered.

"Wait," I said, feeling in the pocket of my purple suede vest, "I have something in here." I pulled out a partly crumpled piece of paper. As I started to smooth it out, some printing on one side caught my eye.

I heard Alex gasp from across the table.

I looked up at her. She was staring at the paper in my hands.

"Are you thinking what I'm thinking?" I asked, my heart beating rapidly in my chest.

"I sure am," she replied. Her face was pale.

"The surveyors!" we cried at the same time.

"What are you talking about?" Becca asked.

"Surveyors? What surveyors?" Kayla asked.

"What's going on?" Carson wanted to know. "Did I miss something?"

"If you did, then I did, too," Becca reassured her.

I took a deep breath. "I found this on the red trail that day when Alex and I were fixing the markers there," I said, indicating the paper in my hands. "It's some kind of receipt or something from a land surveyor." I turned to Alex. "You can probably explain it better than I can."

"Actually, I think it's a surveyor's worksheet," Alex said. "It must have been left by some surveyors up on the trail. They were up there taking measurements of the landscape, possibly for a construction project of some kind." Her big brown eyes grew serious. "*And* we found it on the part of the trail that overlooks Mill Valley."

"Wait a minute," Becca said excitedly. "Don't surveyors work with that funny equipment on tripods? You know, those things that look like cameras?"

Alex nodded. "Why? Did you see someone in the park like that?"

"Sophie and I both did!" Becca cried. "Remember, Sophie? When we were hiking by the river that day? Right after we found the old mill, we heard voices."

"Sure!" I said, remembering. "We thought they were taking pictures. They were on a trail just above us. I guess it must have been the red trail."

"Then that's it!" Kayla cried. "Mr. Cramson must have hired the surveyors. He must be planning to build something in Mill Valley. *That's* what he needs the land for!"

"Is Cramson's name anywhere on that paper?" Alex asked me eagerly.

I unfolded the rest of the paper and scanned it.

"No," I said, disappointed. "There's no name at all. Just 'Sansevere Land Surveyors.' Here, see for yourself."

"But they must have been working for *someone*," Alex insisted, taking the paper. "Okay, here it is. Client number 198237."

"*That* doesn't tell us much," Becca said, disappointment in her voice.

"No, but that number must stand for *somebody,*" Alex pointed out. "The question is, is that somebody Mr. Cramson?" She grinned. "And I think I may have a way we can find out."

NINE

Ten minutes later, the five of us stood in the entrance vestibule to the Cayenga Grill, gathered around the pay telephone there.

"Do you think it will work?" Carson asked doubtfully.

"Of course it will work," Becca said, a twinkle in her green eyes. "It's a great plan, Alex."

Alex looked around the group. "Okay," she said, "who wants to make the phone call?"

"Don't you want to?" I asked.

Alex shook her head nervously. "Not if I don't have to."

I was surprised. "Are you sure? After all, it was your idea."

Alex grinned. "*Ideas* are no problem for me, Sophie. But *acting,* that's a different story."

"I don't think I'd better do it, either," Kayla said. "Whenever I try to fool anyone my voice starts shaking."

"I'll do it," I volunteered.

"That's brave, Sophie," Becca said.

I shrugged. "I like this kind of stuff," I said with a grin. "Besides, I'll do anything to help the Double-L," I added more seriously. I turned to Alex. "Just tell me what to say again, okay?"

Quickly, Alex went over the plan with me once more.

"Okay," I said. I could feel my heart pumping a little faster with anticipation. "Who has a quarter?"

"I do," Carson volunteered.

I inserted Carson's coin into the telephone and dialed the telephone number for Sansevere Land Surveyors from the piece of paper in my hand.

After two rings, a woman picked up. "Good afternoon. Sansevere."

I took a deep breath. *Just stay calm and believe what you're saying,* I reminded myself. *If you believe it, then she'll believe it.*

"Yes," I began. "I'm calling about a bill from your company for a surveying job over in Cayenga Park. My client number is"—I paused and glanced down at the paper in my hand—"198237."

"Why certainly," the woman said. "Let me just look that up in our computer system for you." I could hear the rapid click of computer keys in the background. "Oh, yes, here we are. Nosmarc Flo-Dur, is that right?"

"What?" I asked, confused.

"Nosmarc Flo-Dur," she repeated. "That's the name on the account."

"Are you sure?" I asked, flustered. "I mean, are you sure it isn't Cramson?"

"No," she said, sounding a little surprised. "It says right here, 'Nosmarc Flo-Dur Waterworks.' That's *N, O, S, M, A, R, C* . . . *F, L, O, dash, D, U, R*. Why? Isn't that correct?"

"No, no, I guess that's it," I answered quickly. "Okay, then, thank you very much."

"Wait a minute," the woman said. "I thought you said you were calling about a problem with your bill."

"Un, no, that's okay," I said, stammering a little. "The problem's all cleared up now. Thanks anyway." I hung up.

"What happened?" Kayla asked. "Wasn't Mr. Cramson the one they did the job for?"

I shook my head. "No. They said it was for some other company. Nosmarc Flo-something-or-other."

"Are you sure you got the client number right, Sophie?" Alex asked.

"Definitely," I answered. "I read it right off this piece of paper."

"Then I guess it *wasn't* Mr. Cramson the surveyors were working for after all," Carson said.

Becca looked disappointed. "But it *had* to be him. We had it all worked out."

Alex sighed. "Yeah. Unfortunately, however, it seems as though we had it all worked out *wrong*."

• • •

When I arrived at the ranch the following afternoon, Matt greeted me with a huge smile.

"Sophie, hi!" he said. "I'm so glad to see you. Wait until I tell you what's been happening around here during the past week! You won't believe it!"

"Hi, Matt," I said, returning his smile. "What's up?"

"Business, that's what," Matt said happily. "All of a sudden we've had a whole bunch of people come by wanting to rent horses to see the park."

"That's terrific, Matt," I said, my smile growing even broader.

He looked at me, his green eyes narrowing. "Hang on a minute. You had something to do with this, didn't you?"

I laughed. "I'm so happy it worked!"

"What worked?" Matt asked. "What did you do, Sophie?"

"Just a little advertising," I replied. "GIRLS R.U.L.E. style, that is."

"What?" Matt looked confused.

"The rest of the girls in the junior rangers and I have been telling people we see in the park about the ranch," I explained. "You know, suggesting to them that they might want to think about taking out a horse and seeing the park on horseback."

Matt's eyes were shining. "You did that for us, Sophie?"

"Sure," I answered. "For you, and Rosemary, and Blizzard, and Chocolate, and all the rest of the horses." My eyes met his. "I don't want to see your family lose the ranch, Matt."

"Thanks, Sophie," Matt said. "Maybe we have a chance now, if we can keep it up. I really appreciate it. And I know my grandparents will, too, when they find out it was you." He grinned. "Boy, when you said you wanted to help out around the ranch I had no idea you meant like this."

I laughed. "Hey, don't let me off that easy, Matt," I joked. "I still expect you to make me muck out the stalls, clean the tack, groom and feed the horses, and all that other stuff."

Matt laughed, too. "You've got a deal."

Just then I spotted two men headed our way up the dirt road.

"Looks like you might have some more customers," I said, nodding toward them.

Matt turned to look at them.

"Oh, yeah," he said, nodding. "I recognize those guys. They were here last Sunday evening."

"Sunday, huh?" I said, a little surprised. I grinned. "Well, I guess those are two customers I can't take credit for, Matt, seeing as GIRLS R.U.L.E. didn't start our advertising campaign until Tuesday."

As the men approached, I could see that one was short and heavy, with thick black hair and a mustache. The other one was tall and balding. They both wore dark blue jeans that looked brand new, and carried backpacks. I also noticed that they both wore shiny dark shoes that seemed unusual for riding. They were the kind of shoes that men usually wear with suits.

"Hi, there!" Matt greeted them warmly. "Came back for another ride, huh?"

"That's right," the taller man answered quickly. "We'd like to take those two horses out again."

"Rosemary and Brownie," Matt said with a nod. "Sure. I'll have them saddled up for you in just a moment. Will you be needing a guide this time? I'd be happy to show you some of the more scenic trails if you—"

"No, no, that's all right," the short man cut him off. "I mean, thank you very much anyway. I think we'll do okay on our own."

"Okay then, I'll just get the horses," Matt said.

"I'll help you, Matt," I volunteered.

A few minutes later, Matt led Brownie, a smallish brown stallion, down from the stable, with Rosemary and me right behind him.

We held the horses as the two men struggled into the saddles. Watching them, it was clear even to me that they didn't have much experience riding. And those packs on their backs weren't making it any easier.

I caught Matt's eye and he gave me an amused wink. All of a sudden I felt like I was going to laugh. Something about the sight of those two men in their shiny shoes and their backpacks trying to get onto the horses just struck me as hilariously funny. I turned away and held my breath.

It definitely would not be good for the Flynns' business to start laughing at the customers, I reminded myself. But it was all I could do to control myself. And even without looking at him I could tell that Matt was standing beside me feeling the exact same way.

Finally, as the men made their way unevenly on their

horses down the dirt road toward the trailheads, I turned to look at Matt. The two of us burst out laughing.

"Kind of makes *you* feel like a pro, I bet," Matt said, his eyes wrinkling at the corners.

"I'll say," I agreed, trying to catch my breath. I shook my head. "Matt, I don't want to be mean, but those two guys must be the worst riders in the world."

"I know," Matt replied. He grinned at me. "Imagine what would have happened if I'd given them some feisty horses, like Pepper and Silver."

"Or Blizzard!" I added.

Matt laughed. Then he sighed. "Well, Rosemary and Brownie should take care of them okay, anyway." He turned to me. "You still want to make good on that promise to help me muck out the stalls?"

"I'm good for my word," I replied.

"Okay, then, let's go," Matt said, heading to the stable.

TEN

Because I'm dreaming,
Dreaming green . . .
Hope you catch my meaning,
Dreaming green . . .
Dreaming green . . .
Dreaming green . . .

As the clock-radio alarm went off in my room the following morning, I woke up to one of my favorite songs. It was actually the song that had been playing on Matt's earphones the very first time I met him, "Dreaming Green" by Pop Quiz. *It's hard to believe that was only a week ago,* I thought. *Somehow I feel like I've known Matt a lot longer.*

I rolled over in bed. Lemonade lifted her head from the rug and thumped her tail hopefully.

I yawned and looked at the clock radio. Eight o'clock. Getting up early on Saturday mornings definitely isn't one of my favorite things about working in the park. But Saturday's a busy day for visitors, and Ranger Abe likes to meet with both divisions of the junior rangers early so we can get out there and start on our assignments.

Lemonade began to whimper a little.

"Okay, okay, Lem, I'll let you out in a minute," I promised. I stretched lazily under the covers.

The song on the radio came to an end, and the DJ came on.

"That was 'Dreaming Green,' from the new one by Pop Quiz. You're listening to WCCC, the radio station of Cayenga County College, and I'm Mick Jones. Coming up, we have the Strawberries, Flying Angel, and Alyssa Raith. But first an update on the water situation."

I sat up in bed immediately. *The water situation? What water situation?* I wondered.

Lemonade, even more hopeful now, wandered over and stuck her cold nose against my leg.

"Just a minute, girl," I told her, scratching her behind the ears. "Let me listen to this."

"As I reported earlier, we have a full Water Warning for the Cayenga County area this morning. Potentially dangerous levels of chlorine were found during a routine test of the Cayenga Park reservoir yet again. Tests from the same location prompted the Health Department to declare a Water Alert just five days ago. Today's levels were even higher, causing the increase from 'Alert' to 'Warning.' Officials are cautioning that no one should drink Cayenga County tap water until this problem has been taken care of."

I couldn't believe my ears. *This definitely sounds a lot more serious than last time,* I realized. I jumped out of bed.

Lemonade, thrilled that I was up at last, let out a bark.

"Don't worry, Lem, I'm in a hurry, too," I told her. As fast as I could began to pull clothes out of my bureau drawers and throw them on. A minute earlier, I'd been tired, but now I felt full of energy. All I wanted to do was get to the park as soon as I could and see what I could find out for myself.

As I approached the North Entrance to the park, I almost couldn't believe my eyes. Tacked to the large wooden WELCOME TO CAYENGA PARK sign was another sign—a paper sign with hastily scrawled letters:

- CAMPGROUND
- RESERVOIR BOATING
- MOUNTAIN CENTER
- KIDDIE BEACH & POOL
- PARK SNACK BARS

ALL <u>CLOSED</u> TODAY DUE TO HEALTH DEPT.
WATER WARNING

PLEASE BRING YOUR <u>OWN</u> DRINKING WATER INTO
THE PARK!! ALL FOUNTAINS AND REST ROOM
SINKS HAVE BEEN TEMPORARILY SHUT DOWN.

THANK YOU.

This is terrible! I thought. *How could something like this be happening?* I knew that an awful lot of park visitors were going to be disappointed when they arrived and saw this.

I quickly made my way over to Park Headquarters. Even though I was about twenty minutes early, a bunch of junior rangers had gathered there already, including Alex, Carson, and Kayla.

I sat down beside the three of them. They were talking with Walker and Kevin of the boys' division. They all greeted me briefly and went back to their conversation.

"My dad heard someone on television this morning who said the problem might even be from the old mill up on the river," Walker was saying, a concerned expression on his face.

"What do you mean?" Carson asked. "It's chlorine, right? Like they use in swimming pools. What could the old mill have to do with something like that?"

"Something about chemicals the mill used to use back when it was working," Walker said with a shrug. "I don't really know, exactly."

Kevin shook his head. "That sounds weird to me."

"Well . . . ," Alex began.

We all turned toward her.

"Chlorine *is* a waste product of paper mills," Alex said. "They use it to bleach the paper. At one time the old mill probably *was* dumping its chlorine right into the river."

"Yuck!" Kayla said. "That's disgusting!"

"Wait a minute, though," Carson pointed out, "the river

102

doesn't even feed into the reservoir. How could chlorine that was dumped into the river be getting into the reservoir?"

Alex shrugged. "Factories and mills dispose of toxic stuff in lots of different ways. It's possible they even *buried* some of the chlorine near the mill. It might take a long time, even years, for it to seep into the groundwater from there. But once that happened anything nearby could be affected—including the reservoir. Although I'd say chances are the chlorine would have broken down into some other substance by now. But anything's possible."

Just then Becca came into the room. Her short hair was tousled, and her face was flushed. She didn't even have a smile on her face, which was definitely pretty unusual for her.

"Hi, you guys," she said, crossing quickly to where we were sitting. She sat down in a chair. "Boy, my mom and Barry are totally losing it over this Water Warning thing. Barry can't cook without water! That means they're going to have to keep the restaurant closed until the Health Department lifts the ban."

"I guess they're going to lose a lot of business," I said sympathetically.

Becca nodded. "Saturday's usually their biggest night of the week."

We were interrupted by the sound of Ranger Abe's voice as he came into the room.

"Junior rangers," he said in a brisk and serious tone, "I'm glad to see you all here on time. We have a difficult situation to handle here today, as most of you probably know. I've put extra rangers on staff as well, but I'm going to need each one of you to do your best to help out."

There was a murmur from the room as we all assured Ranger Abe that we would.

"We've got several areas of the park that are off-limits to visitors today," Ranger Abe continued, consulting his clipboard. "The campground, the Mountain Center, the kiddie beach and pool, and of course the reservoir boating facility are all closed. In addition, the snack bars will not be operating. Finally, the water supply to all the water fountains and rest rooms sinks have been shut off."

Kayla raised her hand. "I was just thinking. Since visitors are going to be bringing their own bottled water into the park, we should all probably be on the lookout for extra litter, right?"

Ranger Abe nodded. "Good point, Kayla. Everyone watch for people discarding empty bottles on the trails and in other areas of the park." He sighed heavily. "Frankly, kids, I don't know how long we're going to be able to keep the park open if this warning isn't lifted."

There were several gasps.

"You really might have to close the park?" Carson said incredulously.

"I know, it would be a real shame," Ranger Abe replied. "But we can't operate for long without a supply of drinking water. From what I hear, the county is planning to temporarily shut off the portion of the town's water supply that comes from our reservoir. That means that people in town will have limited water, but up here in the park we won't have any."

I thought of something and raised my hand. "What about the people who live on private land inside the park?" I asked. "Over in Mill Valley? There's the Double-L Ranch, and the Busy Bee, and the vineyard. How are they going to get water?"

Ranger Abe shook his head. "I'm afraid not much can be done for them," he said. "They're going to have to survive on bottled water until this thing clears up." He paused. "*If* it clears up. From what I hear, if this keeps up the county's thinking of closing down the reservoir and putting in a whole new water system. They've been talking with some new company in town, Nosmarc Flo-Dur, about doing the job."

I froze. *Nosmarc Flo-Dur? Where have I heard that name before?*

Beside me, Alex nudged me hard in the arm. I turned to look at her. Her brown eyes were wide. "Nosmarc—isn't that the name of the company that the woman at Sansevere gave you when you called?"

"Oh my gosh, it is!" I gasped.

"Are you sure?" Kayla asked, overhearing us.

I nodded. "I remember. She even spelled it for me."

I saw Kayla turn to Becca and Carson to explain what was happening.

"What do you think this means?" I asked Alex.

"I don't know," Alex replied under her breath. "But I don't like the sound of it. I'd say there's definitely something very strange going on here."

I couldn't have agreed more.

ELEVEN

Later that afternoon, the five members of GIRLS R.U.L.E.
gathered at Park Headquarters to sign out on the board. As
I gazed around at Kayla, Becca, Carson, and Alex, they all
seemed as exhausted as I was. Saturday is usually our
busiest day in the park, anyway. But this Saturday had been
the toughest by far.

A lot of visitors must have changed their minds about
coming to the park once they found out about the water and
the closings. But even though there had been a lot fewer
visitors than usual, the ones who had shown up were pretty
confused and full of questions about the Water Warning,
which meant that there was a lot for us to do. And, as
Kayla had warned us, there were quite a few problems with
people leaving empty water containers on the trails and in
the public areas.

"Phew! What a day!" Carson said, wiping her forehead with the sleeve of her white sweatshirt.

"You can say that again," Kayla agreed.

"You guys, listen," Alex said intently. "I know we're all tired, but I think we should put our heads together and do a little more investigating on this Nosmarc thing."

"What kind of investigating?" I asked with interest.

"I'm not exactly sure," Alex replied. "But we could start with just a little general snooping around, for one thing."

Carson sighed. "I don't know if I have any energy left for snooping, Alex. My feet are killing me."

Alex grinned. "The kind of snooping I have in mind won't bother your feet at all, Carson."

"So you *do* have a bed and not just a bike, after all, Alex," Becca joked.

"Wow, nice room," Kayla said appreciatively.

I didn't say anything at all. I was too busy looking around the enormous pink and beige room. Alex had the hugest bedroom—and the hugest house—I had ever seen. The house was high on a cliff, and there was even a view of the ocean from Alex's room. I couldn't imagine what it must be like to live in a place like that.

"Thanks," Alex said with a little shrug. "I'd like it a lot more if my parents would let me keep it the way I want."

"What do you mean?" Carson asked.

"You know, if I could get rid of all this decorator stuff," Alex replied with a sweep of her hand. "I hate pink and white"—she made a face—"excuse me, I mean *salmon* and *cream*; that's what the decorator calls it." She sighed. "But my parents had the whole house redone a couple of months ago, and this is what I got."

"You're kidding," I said incredulously. "You mean they won't even let you decorate your own room?"

Alex laughed. "I guess they're worried I'd make the place look like a mechanic's garage, or some inventor's workshop or something, and it wouldn't go with the rest of the house. And they're probably right."

I didn't say anything. I couldn't imagine my room at home without my own special touches—my Flying Angel and Alyssa Raith posters, the collage my friend Miranda made me for my birthday last year, my patchwork quilt, and my rag rug. I felt sorry for Alex.

Alex kicked off her hiking boots and sent them flying across the room. She tossed her backpack on her bed, which was covered with a salmon-pink spread. "Just throw your stuff anywhere, guys," she invited. "I'll get started."

Alex took a seat at a pale wood desk opposite the bed. On the desk was a computer with a huge monitor, along with a scanner, a printer, speakers, and a bunch of other computer equipment I didn't even recognize.

There were two matching beige silk-covered chairs by another window. I grabbed one, and Carson took the other. We brought them over to the desk and sat down on either side of Alex. Becca and Kayla settled themselves on the nearby window seat.

I waited as Alex began to type on the keyboard and click

the mouse. It was pretty clear watching her that she knew her way around a computer about as well as Carson knew her way around the park.

After a few moments, Alex looked up. "Well, I found the Nosmarc Flo-Dur home page on the Web," she announced.

"They have one?" I asked, leaning forward to peer at the screen.

"Most companies do," Alex informed me. "It's pretty much just another way of advertising. But maybe it will have some important information."

"Let's learn more about Nosmarc Flo-Dur," Kayla suggested, pointing at the screen.

"Sounds like a good place to start," Alex agreed. She clicked the mouse, and the image on the screen changed. *"Nosmarc Flo-Dur is a premium name in water processing and filtration systems,"* she read. *"Nosmarc Flo-Dur Waterworks projects supply water to communities throughout the California area, as well as to neighboring states. Our state-of-the-art facilities employ the lastest technologies to provide clean, plentiful, drinkable tap water wherever it may be needed."*

"Well, that sure tells us a lot," Becca joked from her spot on the window seat.

"You weren't kidding when you said these web pages were basically advertisements," Kayla agreed. "I feel like I'm listening to a commercial on TV."

"Let's try 'Visit Nosmarc Flo-Dur Waterworks projects sites,'" Alex decided, clicking the mouse.

"There sure are a lot of project locations," Carson said,

NOSMARC FLO-DUR

WATERSYSTEMS

**MAIN OFFICE: 2735 COMMERCE STREET
SAN PEDRA**

Click below to:

> *Learn more about Nosmarc
> Flo-Dur Watersystems*

> *Visit Nosmarc Flo-Dur
> Waterworks projects sites*

> *Obtain regional
> Office Address*

> *Get information about this
> web page*

gazing at the screen. "Look at this—San Pedro, Richfield, Santa Maria, Viejo . . . they've even got a project in Puma, Arizona."

"Puma, Arizona!" Kayla exclaimed. "My cousins live near there. That's practically in the middle of a desert."

"I wonder how they manage to supply water *there,*" Alex said thoughtfully. "Let's take a look." She clicked the mouse.

A moment later, an image of a large body of water filled the screen. I squinted to see the caption underneath the photograph.

"Nosmarc Flo-Dur water storage facility, Puma, Arizona," I read. "It looks like a lake."

"It's definitely not a lake if it's in the middle of the desert," Alex pointed out. "At least, not a natural lake." She started clicking her mouse. "Let's look at a map and see what kind of water source might be near there."

A few moments later, a map appeared on the screen.

"There's our answer," Alex said triumphantly. "They diverted the river to flood the Puma Canyon and create a reservoir."

Carson made a face. "Can you really drink *river* water like that? I thought tap water usually came from rainwater."

"Sometimes it does and sometimes it doesn't," Alex answered, clicking back to the image of the desert lake. "Just about any water can be made drinkable if it's properly cleaned and treated. Sometimes treating it involves a lot of chemicals, though."

"Yuck," Kayla said. "I'd rather drink water than chemicals any day."

"The question is, what does any of this have to do with those surveyors who were in the park that day?" I wondered out loud.

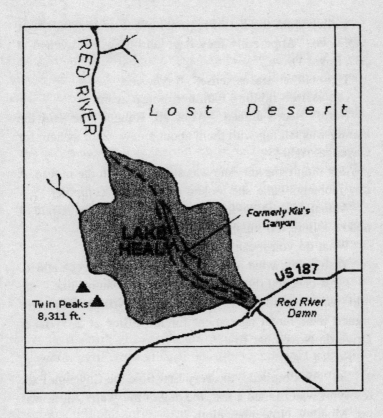

"Well, let's see what else we can find out," Alex replied, playing with the mouse.

"Hey, look," Carson exclaimed, pointing to the screen. "It says 'Cayenga.'"

"Really?" Becca said. "Where?" She and Kayla walked over.

"I clicked on the list of regional office addresses," Alex explained. "Apparently they have an office in Cayenga at 237 Baker Drive."

"I guess that makes sense," Kayla said.

Alex started fiddling with her mouse again.

"Sure," Becca agreed. "After all, Ranger Abe said the county was talking with them about a new water system for Cayenga, right?"

Alex didn't answer. She was still busy with the mouse. A few moments later, she looked up from the computer.

"Actually," she said, her voice serious, "I'm afraid it makes a little too much sense."

"What do you mean?" I asked anxiously.

"Yeah, Alex, what are you talking about?" Becca added.

"I just checked the County Records Bureau on-line," she told us. "According to their records, Nosmarc Flo-Dur signed their rental agreement for the office at 237 Baker Drive on November first."

"So?" I said.

"So," Alex replied, "the very first time the Cayenga Park reservoir water failed a test, the day of the Water Alert, was last Monday, November ninth."

"Oh wow," I said, understanding.

"That was only eight days later," Kayla added.

"I guess that's a pretty big coincidence, huh?" Carson said.

"Yeah," Alex replied. "A little *too* big, if you ask me."

TWELVE

The following afternoon as I approached the North Entrance to the park, I was startled by a new sign.

```
SORRY—

PARK CLOSED UNTIL FURTHER NOTICE DUE TO
WATER SHUTOFF
```

I couldn't believe it. The park had never been closed— not ever in my whole life! I glanced at the welcome booth and saw a figure in a ranger uniform sitting inside. Feeling sort of numb, I walked over to the booth.

As I got closer I recognized the ranger as Carson's mother.

Ranger McDonald was reading a book, but she looked up as I approached.

"Hi, Sophie," she said.

"Hi, Ranger McDonald," I greeted her. "Is it really true? Is the park closed today?"

"I'm afraid so," she replied. "The county shut off the water up here. We can't operate a park without any water."

"Can I still go in?" I asked hopefully. "I'm supposed to visit someone who lives in Mill Valley."

"Sure, Sophie, go ahead," Ranger McDonald said. "Just stick to the main roads and don't go on any of the back trails. We don't have much staff here today."

"Okay, sure," I agreed.

A little while later, as I made my way up the dirt road toward the ranch, I was surprised to see Matt and his grandmother leading several of the horses down the path toward me.

I waved, and Matt waved back to me. A few moments later, we all met on the road.

"Hi, Sophie," Matt said with a smile.

"Hi, Matt. Hi, Lulu," I replied.

"I'm glad you're here, Sophie," Lulu said. "Good timing, my dear. Would you mind taking Pepper and Rosemary for me so I can go back to the house? I've got to take Matt's grandpa into town to have his leg checked. They may be taking the cast off in the next couple of days, and Lester's so anxious to get rid of that thing I'm afraid he may try to walk into town on his own!"

"Sure, I'll be happy to," I volunteered.

She handed me the reins for the two horses. "I'll see you both a little later."

"Okay, bye, Gran," Matt called after her. "Don't forget to pick up more bottled water while you're in town!"

"I'll get as much as I can fit in the trunk!" she called back, heading toward the house.

"Hi, Rosemary. Hi, Pepper," I greeted the horses. I turned to Matt. "Hey, where are we taking them, anyway?"

"To the river," Matt replied. "They need to drink."

"Oh, right," I said. I hadn't thought about that. *Of course the Flynns can't be giving all the horses bottled water,* I realized. *They'd need to buy about a ton of it a day.* "I guess it's a good thing the river's close by."

"You can say that again," Matt said. "I don't know what we'd do without it. We have no water here today, you know."

I nodded. "That must be really hard."

Matt sighed. "It's terrible for business. You can't exactly get many customers when the park's closed."

"Matt, I feel so bad," I said. "I can't believe this happened, especially just when things were starting to look better for the ranch."

We approached the river and let the horses drink.

"I just hope they get the reservoir opened up again soon," Matt said. "It's not going to be easy for us living on bottled water and walking the horses down here to drink three times a day."

"Didn't you hear, Matt?" I asked. "They're thinking of keeping the reservoir closed for good."

"But they can't do that!" Matt objected. "That reservoir is a major water supplier for the whole county, isn't it?"

"I heard that the county is talking about having some company called Nosmarc Flo-Dur build a new waterworks system," I explained.

"What are we supposed to do while they're building that?" Matt exploded. "The ranch can't survive without water." He shook his head. "Forget it. They can't do it. My grandparents aren't the only people living in Mill Valley. They can't just turn off everyone's water like that, right?"

"I hate to tell you this, Matt," I said, "but the way things are going, it looks like soon your grandparents might end up being the only people living in Mill Valley after all."

"What are you talking about?" he asked.

Quickly I explained to him about Becca and my visit to the apiary and the vineyard.

"You mean everyone's going to sell their land to Rudolf Cramson?" Matt asked incredulously.

"It kind of looks that way," I said. "The beekeepers, Stephanie and Will, don't really want to. They said they'd stay if business were just a little better. And Becca and I got the feeling that the Consuelo brothers are mostly interested because they think they can get a high price for their land from Mr. Cramson."

"Well, that's not too likely anymore," Matt pointed out. "No one's about to pay a lot for a place with no water supply there."

I shrugged. "They seem to think there must be gold or

something else in their land, since Mr. Cramson wants it so much."

"I wonder why Cramson *does* want all our land?" Matt said thoughtfully.

I shook my head. "I've been asking myself that same question for days," I said.

"Quién es la madre de Carlos?" Senora Flores asked, reading aloud the question from the book.

"Senora Nunez es la madre de Carlos," Kendra Lewis, the girl sitting to my right, responded.

"Bueno," the teacher complimented her. "Sophie? Next question?" She read from the book. *"Qué hace Carlos después de escuela?"*

What does Carlos do after school? I translated silently. I quickly scanned the story directly above the questions in my Spanish book.

"Carlos camina a su casa con su amigo, Ricardo," I answered. I held back a yawn. Sometimes Spanish class could be so boring. *Who cares whether Carlos walks home with his friend Ricardo after school?* I thought. *Why can't Carlos ever do anything interesting, like go hang-gliding, or start a rock band?*

It was Monday afternoon, and I was sitting in my last class of the day, Spanish with Senora Flores. Spanish has always been pretty easy for me, and going around the classroom like this, taking turns answering questions from the book, is definitely not my idea of an exciting activity.

I glanced at the clock. Ten minutes left of class. As

Michael Dunn, the boy sitting to my left, struggled with the next question, I opened my notebook and began to doodle.

First I wrote my name in fancy script.

Sophie Schultz

Then I wrote Matt's name the same way.

Matt Flynn

Hey, that looks pretty good, I decided, admiring my work. I tried to think of something else to write.

The Double-L Ranch

That one looks great, I thought. *Maybe I should make some kind of sign or something for the Flynns like that.*

I thought again about the story Matt had told me about the Double-L, and how it had gotten its name from his grandparents' names, Lulu and Lester. What was it Matt had said? That finding each other was all the luck his grandparents said they ever needed. That was so sweet.

That ranch just has to stay in Matt's family, I thought angrily. *They can't let it get into the hands of Mr. Cramson. Without Lulu and Lester, the whole story of the naming of the Double-L won't even have any meaning anymore.*

I began scratching angrily in my notebook. Before I knew it, I had written Cramson's name in big, ugly block letters.

CRAMSON

Just looking at the name on the page in front of me made me feel angry. *I wonder who this Cramson guy is anyway and what he's like,* I thought. *What could he possibly want with a ranch, an apiary, and a vineyard—especially ones that aren't even doing well?*

Then, suddenly, I noticed something that made my heart stop.

"Oh my gosh!" I gasped, staring down at the paper in front of me.

"Sophie?" Senora Flores said inquiringly. *"Qué pasa contigo?"*

Oh, nothing. I mean *nada,"* I said quickly, covering up the doodles in my notebook. But something definitely was happening—something I almost couldn't believe myself.

The bell rang, signaling the end of class. Around me, students jumped up from their desks and headed for the door.

But not me. I was too busy rearranging the letters in my notebook.

CRAMSON

NOSMARC

I couldn't believe my eyes. I thought hard. *What did Matt say Mr. Cramson's first name was? He mentioned it to me just yesterday, I'm sure of it.* Then I remembered—*of course! What else could it be?* It made perfect sense. Too much sense, as Alex would say.

I quickly scribbled in my notebook. My palms were sweaty. And a terrible chill of recognition ran up my spine as I stared down at the words in front of me.

RUDOLF CRAMSON = NOSMARC FLO-DUR

THIRTEEN

The moment I left the school building, I started running. I ran straight home and flew up the stairs to my room, with Lemonade at my heels. Ignoring her, I started pulling clothes out of everywhere—my drawers, my closet, even the hamper—and searching through the pockets.

Where is that thing? I thought with frustration. *I know I had it in my pocket that afternoon at the Cayenga Grill.* Then I had a terrible thought. *What if I left it at the restaurant?*

Calm down, Sophie, I told myself. *Calm down and think.* I looked around the room. Clothes were strewn everywhere, and Lemonade was cowering in a corner, eyeing me with distrust.

What was I wearing that afternoon at the restaurant? I tried hard to think. *Whatever it was, I had it on that day at the park, too,* I realized, *the day I first found the paper on the trail.*

Then, suddenly, I remembered. *My purple suede vest!*

But where is that? I ran to my closet. It wasn't there. Then I spotted it draped over the back of my old wooden rocking chair. I grabbed it. Sure enough, the paper was inside the pocket, just where I'd left it.

I stuffed the paper into the pocket of the orange and lime-green checked minidress I was wearing and made for the stairs again. As I hurried down, I almost bumped straight into my mother on her way up.

"Mom!" I cried in surprise. "What are you doing home?"

"It was slow today at the hospital, so they let me leave early," she replied. "I thought I'd make a nice home-cooked dinner for us all."

"I can't stay," I panted, brushing past her. "I have to go."

"Where are you in such a rush to get to?" she asked.

"The park!" I yelled, continuing down the stairs.

"Wait a minute. You don't work today, do you, Sophie?" she called after me.

"No, but I'll explain later," I said. "I've got to go!"

I raced out to the yard and grabbed my bike. As fast as I could I pedaled out of the driveway and down the road that led to the bike trail.

"Sophie, what's up?" Becca asked.

"I hope this is important," Carson added. "I'm missing a special extra volleyball practice session to be here."

"Your message said it was urgent," Kayla put in.

"Is everything okay?" Alex asked.

It was later that afternoon, and the five of us were standing at the trailhead of the red trail, not far from the base of Mesa del Oro. When I'd discovered that the Water Warning had been reduced to a Water Alert, and that the park was open again, I'd called the other four members of GIRLS R.U.L.E. from a phone at Park Headquarters and told them to meet me right away.

"I made an unbelievable discovery," I told them excitedly now. I reached into the pocket of my dress and pulled out the Sansevere worksheet. "You guys, I know who Client number 198237 is!"

"We all do," Alex pointed out. "Nosmarc Flo-Dur. Why do you think I did all that searching on the computer the other day?"

"Well, there's one thing your search missed, Alex," I said. "Something Nosmarc wasn't exactly advertising on their web page."

"What do you mean?" Carson asked. "What is it?"

"I think I've figured out who's behind the Nosmarc operation," I announced.

"Behind it?" Kayla repeated.

"That's right," I said. "Who the company belongs to. And you won't believe who it is." I looked around at the circle of faces surrounding me. "Rudolf Cramson!"

"Mr. Cramson?" Carson repeated.

"Are you sure?" Becca asked.

"How did you find out?" Kayla wanted to know.

I grinned. "It was all in the names," I said.

Carson was the first to figure out what I meant. "Of course!" she cried. "I get it! 'Cramson' spelled backward is 'Nosmarc'!"

"Did you say Mr. Cramson's first name was Rudolf?" Alex asked eagerly.

"That's right," I replied. "Matt mentioned it yesterday."

"Rud-olf, Flo-dur," Becca said slowly. She shook her head. "I can't believe it. 'Nosmarc Flo-Dur' is 'Rudolf Cramson' spelled backward!"

"What I can't believe is that we didn't notice it sooner!" Alex exclaimed. "Even with all those times I typed Nosmarc into the computer . . ."

"I guess we just weren't looking for it," I said. "It was right under our noses, but we didn't notice it because we were looking for other things." I held up the Sansevere worksheet. "Anyway, now that we do know who's really behind this whole thing, I say we hike up to that ridge where Sansevere did its work and see if we can figure out exactly what it is that Cramson—or Nosmarc—is up to."

"I can't believe this!" Kayla cried with indignation as the five of us stood on the portion of the red trail that overlooked the river, the mill, and the valley.

"This is terrible," Carson agreed.

I nodded grimly. "Nosmarc is obviously trying to do the same thing here that they did in Puma," I said. "Only this time there happen to be people living where they want to make their lake!"

I gazed out at the view. Mill Valley lay before us like a

giant basin, surrounded by mountains. I tried to imagine that basin filled with water. I shuddered and looked away.

Alex was studying the Sansevere worksheet. "All these notations that say 'plus three hundred eighty-seven feet,'" she said. "That must be the measurement of the waterline of the new lake—three hundred eighty-seven feet above sea level."

"Which puts the ranch and the other private property down there pretty far below water," Becca finished.

"And just to make sure the county would agree to the plan, Cramson added his own little special ingredient to the Cayenga Reservoir water supply," I said.

Carson gasped. "Do you really think he poisoned the reservoir?"

"It does seem to make sense," I said. "The Cayenga water supply was fine before that."

"Sophie's got a point," Kayla said. "Cramson knew he'd never get the county to agree to let him build a *new* waterworks plant unless there was some kind of problem with the *old* water supply."

"And he probably had easy access to chlorine from Nosmarc's other waterworks projects," Alex pointed out.

"That's totally illegal!" Becca cried. "He could go to jail for something like that."

"He could, if we could prove it," Kayla pointed out.

"Kayla's right," Alex agreed. "Even if it does make sense, our theory's nothing without proof."

"Well, either way, Rudolf Cramson lied to the Flynns and to those other people, too," I said. "He told them he wanted to keep their businesses running after he took over, but he obviously only said that stuff to make them feel better about selling their land and to keep his real plan a secret until they agreed."

"Right," Becca agreed. "Meanwhile he planned to dump their businesses as soon as he got hold of their land and put the whole valley underwater."

"I bet the Flynns would never agree to sell their ranch if they knew Cramson was going to get rid of their horses," Kayla said.

"You're right, Kayla," I said with determination. "And that's why we have to tell them about it right away. All of them—the Flynns, and Stephanie and Will, and the Consuelo brothers, too. They have to know the truth. And now, before any of them decides to go ahead and sell one single square inch of their land to Rudolf Cramson!"

FOURTEEN

"Matt?" I called, stepping into the cool darkness of the stable. "Matt? Are you there?"

There was no answer. All I heard was the soft whinnying and stamping of some of the horses in their stalls.

"Maybe they're up at the house," Alex suggested.

"Let's check," I agreed.

The five of us had agreed to split up in order to get the news about Cramson's plans to all the Mill Valley residents as quickly as possible. Becca had gone to see the Consuelo brothers at the vineyard, and Kayla and Carson were at the Busy Bee. Alex and I had headed straight for the ranch.

As Alex and I stepped out of the dark stable and into the sunlight again, I was startled by two figures standing directly in front of me.

"Excuse me," the taller of the figures said. "We'd like to take out some horses."

I squinted and recognized the two men who had been there just a couple of days earlier, the ones with the backpacks who'd had so much trouble getting up on their horses. They were dressed the same way today, in their dark jeans and shiny shoes, and they carried their backpacks.

Boy, these two are definitely pretty determined, I thought. *If they keep it up they're going to improve their riding in no time at all.*

"Um, sure," I answered. "You probably need to talk to one of the Flynns, though. Did you check up at the house?"

"Nobody seems to be around," the shorter man said. "Maybe you can help us."

"Yeah," the taller man urged. "You work here, don't you?"

"Well, kind of," I answered.

I thought a moment. *Should I saddle up Rosemary and Brownie for them and let them take them out?* I wondered. *Would the Flynns want me to do that?* In the end, I decided that the Flynns would probably want me to go ahead with anything that meant more business for the ranch.

"Yeah, sure," I said finally. "I'll get the horses for you." I turned to Alex. "Alex, come on in the stable. You can help me."

"Are you sure you know what you're doing, Sophie?" Alex asked in a low voice as we walked back in toward the stalls.

"Pretty sure," I answered. Matt had shown me how to saddle the horses a few times. I was fairly certain I could do it on my own now. "I would bet the Flynns are watering the other horses, and I'm pretty sure they wouldn't want to lose the business."

"You're probably right about that," Alex agreed.

"Anyway, these guys have been here a couple of times before," I explained. "The horses Matt gives them, Rosemary and Brownie, are pretty gentle. They shouldn't give us any trouble." I walked over to Rosemary's stall. "Hi, Rosie. Ready to go out for a ride?"

A few minutes later, with Alex's help, I had harnessed and saddled the horses. I led them out to where the two men were waiting.

"So," I said in a friendly tone, "you guys must have seen a lot of the park by now."

The shorter man turned to me. "What do you mean?" he asked quickly.

"Just that you've taken these horses out a few times now," I replied with a shrug. "You must have seen some pretty nice trails, that's all."

The shorter man narrowed his eyes at me. "You've got a pretty good memory, don't you, kid?"

"Um, I guess," I answered, glancing at Alex.

"Hey, Frank, the kid didn't mean anything by it," the taller man said quickly. "She was just making conversation. Weren't you, kid?"

"Uh, sure," I said. *Of course I was making conversation. What else would I be doing?*

The shorter man eyed me one more time. "Come on, let's go," he said to the taller man.

Alex and I held the horses' reins as the two men struggled

into their saddles. This time, the scene didn't seem funny to me at all. In fact, there was something about these two men that was downright creepy.

I stood beside Alex in silence and watched as they rode down the dirt road toward the trails.

"That was kind of strange," Alex commented.

"It sure was," I agreed, still eyeing the men. They rode unevenly, hanging on to their saddles, their pointy shoes sticking out at awkward angles from the horses' bodies. Their backpacks jostled on their backs as the horses moved.

"They look pretty new at this," Alex said. "You say they've been here before?"

I nodded. "A couple of times. The last time was Friday, I think." I paused, thinking. *Friday. And Matt said they were here once before that, too. When was it?* I struggled to remember the conversation he and I had had when the men last showed up. *Sunday, that was it. I remember that I was surprised to hear there were customers that early, since GIRLS R.U.L.E. didn't start telling people about the ranch until the following Tuesday.*

Suddenly, I had a thought. "Alex," I said quickly, "when was the Water Alert?"

"This past Saturday," she answered. "Remember? We all came to the weekly junior ranger meeting that morning, and Ranger Abe told us all about it."

"No, no, not the Water Warning," I said urgently. "The Water *Alert*. The first one."

"Oh, that was Monday," she answered. "I remember because my sister was supposed to have her tennis lesson that afternoon, and she was all worried about whether or not it would be okay to take a shower in the water."

"Monday, huh? Only one day later," I muttered to myself. "So both times it was one day later."

Alex turned to me. "Sophie, what are you talking about?"

There was no time to answer. I grabbed Alex's arm. "Come on," I yelled. "We've got to follow those two men!"

I started to pull her down the road. Then I shook my head. "Wait a minute. We'll never catch up to them on foot. We'd better take horses." I began pulling Alex the other way, toward the stable.

"Wait, Sophie!" Alex objected. "What is going on? Why do you want to follow those men?"

I looked her in the eye. "Because if I'm right, the future of the reservoir may depend on it!"

FIFTEEN

When Alex and I got back to the paddock, I ran for Rosemary's stall first.

"Oh, right!" I said when I discovered it was empty. "I gave Rosemary to *them*!" I looked around quickly.

"Sophie, I don't think this is such a good idea," Alex said.

"I'm telling you, we have no choice," I insisted. I stopped and looked at her. "Don't you see? Both times that there was a problem with the reservoir water, those two men took horses up into the trails the day before!"

Alex's eyes widened. "You mean you think *they're* the ones poisoning the water?"

"It's just a hunch, but one thing is for sure. Those guys are definitely not typical riders," I pointed out. "They don't even look like they're enjoying themselves. So why do they keep coming back?"

Alex nodded slowly. "And I guess that would account for the weird way that one talked to you just now. Maybe he was afraid you'd figured out what they were up to. But Sophie, don't you think we should call the rangers or the police or something? I mean, maybe it's not safe for us to go up onto the trails after them like this."

"We don't have time," I urged. "By the time anyone else gets here those guys will be way up in the woods. If they're headed up there for the reason I think they are, we've got to follow them and get proof. Come on, help me saddle up a couple of these horses for us."

"Sophie, wait!" Alex's voice sounded very worried now, almost frantic.

I stopped.

"Sophie, I don't know if I can get on a horse," Alex admitted. "I didn't tell you this before, but the reason I stopped my lessons at the country club way back when was that I was scared."

"You, scared?" I almost couldn't believe it. Alex always seemed so sensible and strong, like she wouldn't be afraid of anything. "You? The one who rides her bike down the Dead Man's Peak trail without even touching the handlebars?"

"That's different," Alex said softly. "Bikes are like machines. They're predictable. With an animal you never know what they're going to do next." She shuddered a little. "Especially a big animal like a horse."

"But you were fine when we were saddling them," I pointed out.

"Putting a saddle on a horse is one thing," Alex said. "Actually sitting on top of one is another."

"All right, I'll go by myself," I volunteered.

"No." Alex shook her head. "I can't let you follow those guys on your own. It might be dangerous."

I knew Alex was right. It was a lot safer to travel as a pair.

I remembered the way I'd felt as a little girl when I first got up on that pony at the county fair. "I'll find you a really gentle horse," I promised.

"Okay," Alex said, her voice almost a whisper.

I gazed around the stable. A bunch of the horses were down the road in the paddock, and I knew we didn't have time to bring them in. And I'd already given Rosemary and Brownie to the two men.

"Here," I said, stopping in front of Chocolate's stall. "This one's real sweet. So sweet they named him Chocolate. You take him, and I'll take . . ." My eyes searched the stalls. There was only one horse left. "Oh, my gosh, it's Blizzard," I said under my breath.

"What?" Alex asked.

"Nothing," I said, not wanting to alarm her. I approached Blizzard carefully. "Hi, there, Blizzard." *I wish I had some sugar cubes in my pocket,* I thought. Blizzard had let me groom him and saddle him, but I knew he wasn't used to having anyone but Lester Flynn ride him. The sugar cubes might have helped to convince him.

I knew we had to hurry. Since the two men couldn't ride

well, they'd be traveling slowly. But we still had to make up for their lead before we lost them on the trails forever.

As quickly as we could, Alex and I saddled Chocolate and Blizzard and led them outside. I held Chocolate's reins as Alex climbed cautiously into the saddle.

"You're doing great, Alex," I told her encouragingly.

She nodded silently as I handed her the reins. I noticed that she looked pale.

"Don't worry," I said to her. "Just keep an easy grip on the reins and follow me."

I put a foot into one of Blizzard's stirrups and grabbed hold of the saddle horn. Blizzard shuddered and took a few steps to the side, making me lose my balance.

"Sophie?" Alex said in a worried-sounding voice. "What's wrong with that horse?"

"Nothing," I fibbed. "He'll be find just as soon as I get up on him." I walked toward Blizzard, but he shied away from me.

"Come on, boy," I said encouragingly. "Come on and let me get close." Without realizing it, I'd just repeated a line from one of my favorite Alyssa Raith songs. Reminded of it, I continued humming the melody as I walked toward Blizzard. The horse twitched his ears for a moment and then stood perfectly still.

Does he like my singing? I thought incredulously. *I guess I have heard of music soothing animals before,* I realized. I continued humming. This time Blizzard stood patiently as I pulled myself up into the saddle.

"Okay, here we go," I called to Alex.

She looked worried. "How do I start this thing?"

"Don't do anything for now," I said. "I'll go first with Blizzard, and Chocolate will probably just follow."

I pressed my heel gently into Blizzard's side, and he bucked a little.

"No, no," I said softly. I began to sing in a low voice.

> *Come on and let me get close,*
> *Let's get to know each other note for note.*
> *Stars are shooting and the planets align,*
> *I want to hear the music in your mind.*

Sure enough, Blizzard eased into a gentle trot. I could hear the gentle thud of Chocolate's hooves close behind me.

I twisted in the saddle. "You okay, Alex?"

She nodded, but I could see that she was still pale.

I squinted up ahead of us. We were coming to the trailheads. I decided to take the trail that I knew led up by the reservoir. *After all,* I reasoned, *if those men are planning to poison the water, they'll have to pass that way to do it.*

I eased Blizzard onto the trail, with Chocolate and Alex close behind me. The trees were thick here, and I had to duck a few times to avoid being hit by branches. All the while I kept an eye out for any telltale sign, any movement at all, from among the trees ahead of me.

Finally, I spotted a flash of white ahead and to the right. I slowed Blizzard to a stop and let Chocolate bring Alex up alongside me.

"I think they might be up there," I whispered to Alex, pointing. "I saw something moving."

Alex nodded. "What do you think we should do?"

"Let's ride up a little closer," I suggested. "Maybe we can get a better view."

We guided the horses farther up the trail. As we approached the reservoir, I heard voices. Men's voices.

"I sure hope we don't have to do this again," one of the men was saying. "I'll be happy if this is the last time I ever see a horse in my life."

"Oh, stop complaining, Frank," the other man said. "Remember, if this thing goes through, Cramson's going to give us the top positions in the operation. Believe me, if that happens it'll all be worth it."

Cautiously, I brought Blizzard around the bend and stopped behind a tree as the men came into view. They had tied their horses to another tree and they were bending over their backpacks, fiddling with the buckles and straps. At the sight of them, I let out a little gasp. I turned to Alex.

"Looks like you were right, Sophie," she whispered.

I nodded. "They must be working for Cramson," I whispered back.

"What should we do now?" she asked.

I tried to think. My heart was pounding in my chest. The only thing separating us from these terrible men was a thin veil of leaves. All they had to do to spot us was to turn around.

"Maybe we should head back," I whispered. "Maybe we've heard all we need to prove what they're up to."

Just then, Blizzard began to move beneath me. He shook his mane and let out a soft whinny.

"No, no," I whispered, patting him on the neck. "Quiet down, boy."

But he only became more restless. He stomped his feet and shook his head.

"Blizzard, no," I pleaded, still whispering.

Alex shot me a worried glance.

Softly, ever so softly, I began to sing, my voice shaking with fear.

> *Come on and let me get close,*
> *Let's get to know each other note for note.*
> *Stars are shooting and the planets align,*
> *I want to hear the—*

"What's that?" said one of the men suddenly.

I stopped singing, my heart in my throat.

"Quick, Alex, let's get out of here," I cried. I dug my heel into Blizzard's side and pulled on the left side of the reins, desperately trying to turn him around as fast as I could.

Blizzard reared up on his hind legs and let out a loud whinny. I reached out to try to hold on—to try to find anything I could grab on to. I heard Alex scream beside me as I flew through the air.

SIXTEEN

The next thing I knew, I was down on the ground. My right arm was throbbing, and the faces of the two men were staring down at me.

I winced as the shorter of the two men, the one the tall man had called Frank, twisted my arm behind my back.

"Be quiet," he growled. "And keep moving."

"You, too," the taller man instructed, pushing Alex ahead of him down through the trees.

My heart was pounding. *Where are they taking us?* I wondered. I was terrified, and the pain in my right arm was getting worse. I thought about the horses we had left back by the reservoir. Would they run away? Could it be that someone might find them and figure out that something had happened to us?

Probably not, I realized. *After all, nobody even knows*

that Alex and I gave Rosemary and Brownie to those two men and then took out Blizzard and Chocolate ourselves. Nobody but us, that is.

It took me a few minutes to realize that we were headed downhill, toward the valley and the river. I stumbled, tripping in my sandals as Frank continued pushing me forward. I glanced at Alex. Her face had been scratched by a branch, and her chestnut ponytail had come loose. Her deep brown eyes flashed with anger and fear.

Suddenly I spotted the mill up ahead between some trees.

"Hang on, Joe," Frank said, stopping suddenly. "We'd better make sure no one's around."

The taller man nodded. "I'll check it out." He turned to Alex. "Wait here," he ordered.

Alex didn't say anything.

Frank reached out and grabbed Alex's arm with his free hand. "Don't worry, Joe, they're not going anywhere."

I watched as Joe headed through the woods to the mill and disappeared into the old building. A few moments later he was back.

"It's perfect," he said with an evil grin. "Looks like nobody's been there for years. Nobody likely to stop by in the near future, either."

I felt my throat tighten. *He's right,* I thought, terrified. *Nobody will ever find us in that old mill!* I tried to struggle, but Frank only tightened his grip on me. I winced as a shooting pain went through my arm.

"Hold still!" Frank barked.

"Come on, get moving," Joe commanded.

The two men led us the rest of the way through the woods to the edge of the old mill and pushed us into an open space between two boards in the side of the structure.

I looked around. We were standing in a large, dark, empty room, the same room that Becca and I had peered into that day when we'd first discovered the mill. There was a high ceiling and wooden beams and rafters above us. A rickety-looking wooden staircase against the far wall led up to a small door.

The air inside the big room was cool and damp. It smelled musty. Suddenly a dark shape fluttered down from the ceiling and flew by us.

Alex let out a little gasp.

"It's just a bat," I told her in a low voice. "Becca and I saw them in here earlier."

She nodded silently.

"Come on," Joe said, pulling Alex toward the far wall. He nodded to Frank. "There's a room upstairs where we can put them until we get Cramson."

Joe and Frank pulled Alex and me roughly to the staircase.

"Climb up," Joe ordered.

As Alex and I climbed the rickety stairs, the ancient wood creaked beneath our feet. The two men were close behind us.

I just hope this old staircase holds out, I thought as we neared the small door at the top.

Joe pushed ahead of me and opened the door. Inside was a small, dark room. It seemed almost like a large closet.

At the sight of the tiny, dark space, I froze.

"No, please," I said in a small voice. "Can't we stay out—"

Frank cut me off. "Get in there and keep quiet."

"Wait a minute!" Alex objected.

"Quiet!" Frank barked. "You two have made enough trouble already! Now get in!"

I stumbled into the room behind Alex. The door closed, and I heard the bolt slide into place, sealing the room in complete darkness.

"Alex?" I whispered, my throat dry with fear.

I felt her hand on my arm. "Wait," she whispered back. "They're still out there. Let's listen."

We could hear the men's voices on the other side of the door.

"You think it's okay to leave them there?" Frank asked.

"They're not going anywhere," Joe answered. "That door's locked tight. Come on, let's go get Cramson and see what he wants to do with them."

We heard their footsteps as they went back down the stairs.

"It's really creepy in here," I said to Alex. "I can't see a thing."

"Just wait," Alex said. "The human eye adjusts to darkness in two steps. The first receptors to adjust are the cones. Those are the receptors that give color vision. That adjustment generally happens within the first minute or so. Several minutes later the other eye sensors, the rods, which provide your black-and-white vision, will adjust, too. Then you'll be able to see a lot better."

I almost wanted to laugh. *Only Alex could think of giving a biology lecture at a time like this,* I thought. Still, whatever she had said, she was right. As I waited, the room began to take shape around me. Soon I could see that one of the walls of the room wasn't a wall at all, but a mass of large, rusty metal gears.

"Hey, look at all that stuff!" I said, pointing at the gears. I winced as my arm throbbed again.

"These must be part of the original inner workings of the mill!" Alex said excitedly. She hurried over to a pair of huge upright metal cylinders placed side by side.

Each cylinder was about half Alex's height. Together they looked like two giant metal spools of thread standing next to each other. Vertical dividers separated each spool into narrow compartments, and sticking out from the top and bottom of each of the cylinders were horizontal rows of metal teeth that interlocked.

"Oh, wow!" Alex said appreciatively, gazing at the gears. "This is great!"

"Um, excuse me, Alex, but right now we've got more important things to think about than checking out cool mechanical stuff," I reminded her. "We're locked in here, and those guys could be back with Cramson any minute!"

"I know, I know," Alex said excitedly. "And these gears could be our way out of here!"

"They could?" I asked in amazement. "What do you mean?"

"It depends on whether they still turn," Alex said thoughtfully. "Come on, Sophie, give me a hand."

"Okay, sure," I said, walking over. "What are we going to do?"

"We have to try to budge these things." Alex put her hand up on the top teeth of one of the cylinders. "Ouch! These things are sharp." She looked around for a moment. Then she unbuttoned her flannel shirt and took it off, leaving her white T-shirt on underneath. "Here, help me rip this in half."

Together, we tore her shirt into two pieces.

"Wrap that around your hand," Alex instructed.

I did as she said. We both put our hands against the upper teeth of the cylinder.

"Now, push!" Alex cried.

I leaned into the gear with all my might. A searing pain went through my right arm, and I let out a yelp.

"We have to get you to a doctor," Alex said with concern.

"I'm okay," I said. "I can still push with my other arm."

We tried again. I could feel my sandals slipping on the dirty floor below me.

It's no use, I thought. *This thing probably hasn't moved in about a million years, whatever it is.*

But then, just as I was about to give up, there was a loud creak.

"It's moving!" Alex cried. "Keep pushing!"

Slowly, the large spool began to turn under our weight. As the teeth on the top and bottom interlocked with the teeth of the other spool, that spool rotated as well.

"Okay, stop," Alex said.

We stepped back. I could feel sweat dripping down my face.

"That was great, Alex, but I still don't understand. How's it going to get us out of here?" I asked, breathing hard.

Alex walked over to one of the cylinders and patted the inside of one of the narrow vertical compartments. "We're going to ride one of these to the other side. I'll get in while you turn it, and then when I get to the other side, I'll do the same for you. It'll be almost like a revolving door."

"But Alex, there's no way we'll fit in one those little compartments!" I objected. "They're way too narrow!"

"Remember, each of these compartments matches up with another one on the other cylinder," Alex pointed out. "So there will be twice as much room when they meet up."

"Even so . . ." I looked at the skinny vertical compartment doubtfully.

"We'll be fine," Alex assured me. "Just as long as we pull back as far as we can and stay nice and flat."

"Oh, great," I groaned. "Nice and flat" isn't exactly the best description of my body. Not that I'm incredibly heavy or anything, but I'm definitely more on the round side than the flat side. Then I thought of something. "But what's over there, Alex? What happens when we get to the other side?"

"I don't know," she admitted. "Maybe there'll be a way out, maybe not. But even if it's just another room like this one, it'll be a place to hide from those men until we can get help."

If we ever get help, I added silently. I didn't want to say anything, but it seemed to me like Alex and I could be locked up an awfully long time before anyone thought to look for us here.

"I'll go first," Alex volunteered. She stepped carefully into one of the compartments and backed up as far as she could. "Okay, Sophie, try to turn it."

"Alex, I'm scared," I said. "Too much of you is sticking out. I'm afraid you'll get crushed."

"When the two cylinders meet there will be more room," Alex reminded me. "Just go slow, and I'll tell you if I feel like things are getting too tight."

"Okay." I grabbed onto the compartment divider and took a deep breath. "Here goes."

I leaned into the cylinder, and with all my might, pushed with my one good arm. It was a lot harder without Alex helping me, but we must have loosened something up earlier, when we were pushing together. After a moment, the cylinder began to turn. I watched as Alex's compartment rotated away from me.

"Are you okay?" I called to her, pushing with all my might.

"Fine," came Alex's muffled reply.

Slowly, Alex disappeared from sight. I kept pushing.

A few moments later, I heard her voice from the other side of the cylinder.

"Sophie, I made it! And it looks like there's a way out over here. Come on!" she called.

I stared at the tiny area of the empty compartment in the cylinder. *Can I really fit in there?* I wondered anxiously. *What if I get crushed?*

"Come on!" Alex called again. "It's fine. Don't worry, you'll be okay. Just climb in and back your body up as far as you can. Call to me when you're ready, and I'll start turning."

I hesitated, still staring at the narrow compartment in front of me. Maybe it would be better to stay where I was. *Maybe there's some other way out*, I thought hopefully.

But just then I heard a shout from outside.

"Hurry, Sophie!" Alex urged from the other side of the cylinders. "I think they're coming!"

"Okay, okay!" I called back. I knew I had no choice.

With my heart pounding in my chest, I climbed into the narrow, wedge-shaped compartment. Now that I was inside it seemed smaller than ever. *Don't think about it too much,* I told myself. *Just go for it.*

I squeezed myself into the back of the compartment, trying to make my body as flat and narrow as possible. It was filthy in there, and my arm, which was crushed against the side of the compartment, was really hurting.

"Okay, I'm ready!" I called to Alex, my voice shaking.

"Here goes!" Alex called back.

For a moment nothing happened. I was terrified that the men would come back into the room at any moment and find me there. *Come on, Alex,* I pleaded silently. *Come on!*

Then, slowly, I felt the cylinder begin to move, pulling me around with it like a revolving door. As the two cylinders came together I was enveloped in total darkness. For a moment, I felt panicky. *What if I never get out of here? What if the cylinders get stuck like this?*

But then a tiny, vertical shaft of light opened just to my right. I watched as the column of light grew wider.

"Just stay put until I get you all the way around," she instructed, continuing to push on the gears.

A moment later, to my relief, the compartments separated and I made out Alex's silhouette in front of me.

"Sophie, you did it!" she cried.

I jumped out from the compartment and looked around. We were standing in a room that was similar to the room we had just left, except that this one had a small shuttered window in one wall.

I could hear voices in the distance.

"Alex, we have to hurry!" I cried.

"Come on!" Alex called, pulling me over to the window with her. "Let's see where this leads to."

Together we pried open the shutters. Light from outside streamed into the room. I felt incredibly relieved to be breathing fresh air again. I could hear the sound of the river very close by.

With Alex at my side, I leaned forward to peer out the window. Directly below us was the old waterwheel, and below it, the river.

"Oh, great," I said, my heart sinking. "How are we supposed to get out of here? We can't even dive into the river. It's way too rocky and shallow here. We'd get hurt for sure."

Alex climbed out farther onto the ledge.

"I think there's a way, Sophie," she reported. "There's an old waterway up here, a sluice. Remember, I told you that's what used to make the waterwheel turn? Anyway, there's still water running through it, but if we hang onto the edges we might be able to climb up it and get to the roof."

"Sounds okay to me," I said. Anything sounded better than staying in the old mill, where Cramson and his men were sure to find us any minute.

Alex stood on the ledge. All I could see of her through the window were her dirty jeans and her green suede sneakers. One by one, her legs and feet disappeared as she climbed up.

I poked my head out the window. Alex was directly above me, pulling herself up into what appeared to be a large, curved, wooden slide that ended in a Y shape. Water was running down the slide and pouring off the far arm of the Y to the river below, and Alex's jeans were already soaked up to the thigh.

Ugh, why didn't I wear pants today? I thought, looking down at my grimy orange and green minidress. I eased out of my sandals and slipped them into the two front pockets of my dress. Then I hoisted myself up into the sluice behind Alex, trying to ignore the pain in my arm.

Just then, I heard a man's voice. This time the voice was close by. It was coming from somewhere outside.

Startled, I shifted my position to look around. One of my sandals fell out of my pocket and landed with a splash in the river below.

There was a cry from the woods nearby. "Hey, look! That's them!"

To my horror, I spotted Frank, Joe, and a third man who

I assumed must be Cramson come out of the woods on the far side of the river.

"Up there!" Frank yelled, pointing. "They're getting away!"

"Alex! Hurry!" I cried, scrambling up the sluice behind her.

"Stop them!" Joe yelled. "Quick!" He stepped into the river, followed by the others.

"Alex! They're coming after us!" I wailed frantically.

"Climb fast!" she yelled back.

I gripped the sides of the sluice as hard as I could. My arm was burning with pain and my bare feet were freezing in the icy water. It was almost impossible to keep my balance on the slippery, mossy surface, especially going against the current. Above me, Alex in her sneakers was making only slightly better time.

Meanwhile, the three men were almost across the river. The water was only about waist-high.

"Hurry!" Alex called down to me as she scrambled from the sluice onto the roof.

"I'm trying!" I cried, desperately trying to climb up through the icy water.

"Come on!" one of the men below me yelled. "This way!"

I looked down. To my horror, Joe had crossed the river and was climbing up the waterwheel, using the paddles as steps. Frank and Cramson were close behind him.

"Hurry, Sophie!" Alex urged again. "They're coming! Climb up here!"

She stuck her hand down toward me, and I grabbed hold of it with my good arm. She pulled me up onto the roof.

But the three men were close behind. They were climbing fast, and Joe, who was in the front, had almost made it to the top of the enormous waterwheel.

"We have to find a way down from here before they get up!" Alex said.

She began to run around the roof.

"Oh, Sophie, there isn't any way!" Alex cried from the far end of the roof. "We're stuck up here!"

I looked back toward the waterwheel, trying to think of a way to get down it. But Joe was at the top of the wheel now, his hand reaching for the sluice. I knew the others would reach the top at any moment. For a second I was frozen in place, terrified.

I stared in horror as Joe grabbed at the arm of the sluice where the water was running off it. His hand slipped, and he yelled out a frustrated yelp as he fell back onto the waterwheel. My heart was in my throat.

Joe reached up again, reaching this time for the other arm of the Y, the dry one directly above the waterwheel. As I watched his hand move toward it, I noticed a small trapdoor blocking the flow of water from that arm of the Y, directing it into the other arm and down to the river below.

Suddenly I had an idea. At first I wasn't sure of it. It wasn't the kind of thing I usually figured out on my own. In fact, it was definitely much more the kind of thing that *Alex* usually figured out. But Alex was all the way at the other end of the roof. And there definitely wasn't time to ask her about it.

I decided to take a chance.

Leaning over the edge of the roof, I strained to reach the trapdoor in the sluice. Bracing my good arm against the edge of the sluice to keep from falling, I stretched my hurt arm out as far as it would go. I could feel the pain searing through my arm, but I didn't give up.

Go for it, Sophie, I told myself, trying to ignore the pain. *It's your only hope.*

In one desperate movement, I grabbed hold of the trapdoor and flipped it.

SEVENTEEN

"More chicken coming through! Watch out, everybody!" Lester Flynn called out good-naturedly.

I moved to one side as Matt's grandfather, dressed in a huge red and white checked apron and carrying a big platter of barbecued chicken, came through the yard.

"Lester!" Matt's grandmother called after him. "Take it easy now. You've only had your cast off for a few days, remember that!"

"How long do you have to keep yours on, Sophie?" Carson asked me sympathetically. "Did the doctor tell you?"

I glanced down at my right arm. It was draped in the multicolored scarf I had decided to use in place of the sling the hospital had given me. "Five weeks." I shrugged. "But at least I'm left-handed."

It was five days after the incident at the mill, and the

Flynns were throwing a big barbecue to celebrate. All the girls from GIRLS R.U.L.E. were there, along with the Flynns' Mill Valley neighbors, Ranger Abe, and several other park rangers.

Lester Flynn walked over to me, carrying his platter of chicken.

"Sophie!" he cried, a huge smile on his face. "Have another piece of chicken! It's got my secret recipe barbecue sauce on it."

"Oh, no, thanks, Mr. Fl—I mean Lester," I said. "I've had a bunch of pieces already. I'm full."

"Just let me know if you change your mind," he replied. He winked at me. "The sauce has a new special ingredient this time." He lowered his voice. "Cayenga Blossom Honey. Makes it real sweet and delicious-tasting." He moved on through the crowd.

"He sure does seem happy," Kayla commented.

"Well, with Cramson and his thugs in the hospital and going on to jail after that, he doesn't have to worry about his ranch anymore," Carson pointed out.

"I do feel kind of bad about having injured them so badly," I said.

"Are you kidding, Sophie?" Alex said. "What you did was great! Besides, you had no choice. If you hadn't knocked them into the water like that who knows what they would have done to *us*?"

"I guess you're right," I said.

"Anyway, those guys probably owe GIRLS R.U.L.E. their lives," Becca pointed out. "If Kayla and Carson hadn't found them unconscious downstream and resuscitated them and called an ambulance, they probably wouldn't even have survived at all."

Kayla shook her head. "Good thing I didn't know who they were or what they'd done when we found them or I might not have been able to go through with it."

"Sure you would have," Carson reassured her. "Resuscitating an unconscious person is one of the most important junior ranger responsibilities, no matter who it is. You'd have come through, even if you knew."

"I guess so," Kayla admitted.

"Too bad no one ever found that sandal you said you dropped, though, Sophie," Becca said with a grin.

"What I want to know is how you figured out how to start the waterwheel," Carson said.

I shrugged. "I looked at it and it just made sense. You see, the sluice ended in a Y, like a fork," I explained. "The water was all headed down the far fork, into the river, and bypassing the wheel. I realized that if I just switched the little trapdoor there I could change the direction of the flow of the water to make it turn the wheel. If the wheel started turning, Cramson and his pals wouldn't have a chance of climbing up."

"Meanwhile, I was just running around looking for a way to get off that roof," Alex put in.

Becca laughed. "Sounds to me like you two might have spent a little too much time alone in that mill together. Are you sure when you went through that gear thing that you didn't switch personalities?"

We all laughed.

Just then I saw my mother making her way toward me.

"Mom!" I said in surprise. "What are you doing here?" The Flynns had invited our families, but my mom usually works on Saturday afternoons.

"I decided to take the day off for once," she replied with a smile. "And I'm so glad I did. This place is beautiful."

I smiled back. She looked so relaxed in her jeans and T-shirt, with her hair blowing in the breeze.

"I'm glad you came, Mom," I told her.

"Well, I think I'm going to get some more of that great potato salad," Carson said.

"I'll come with you," Alex offered.

"I guess I'll get some food, too, then," my mother said. "I'll find you again in a few minutes, Soph."

They all walked off toward the picnic tables.

"Hey, look!" Becca said, pointing. "Little Blossom just took some steps!"

Sure enough, Blossom, who looked like a bumblebee in her cute yellow and black striped jumpsuit, was toddling along in the grass, holding on to her father's hands.

"Isn't she sweet?" Kayla said. She squatted down. "Hi, Blossom! Look at you, learning to walk! What a big girl."

The baby cooed appreciatively.

Suddenly, I heard Matt's voice behind me.

"Sophie, there you are."

I turned around. "Hi, Matt."

"Sophie, I really want to say thank you," Matt said

sincerely. "For everything you've done for me and my family."

"I'm just so glad Cramson isn't going to get to carry out his awful plan," I said.

"Me too," Matt agreed. "But there's no chance of that now. None of the Mill Valley residents are going to be selling our land—not for a long time to come."

"Even Stephanie and Will?" I asked. "I thought they wanted to move to the city, for Blossom."

Matt shook his head. "Not anymore. Not now that they discovered that the old mill is technically on their land."

"What?" I said.

"You didn't hear?" Matt asked in surprise. "The old mill belongs to Will and Stephanie. When they bought the apiary, they didn't realize the mill came with it. Now that they know they've decided to fix it up and start a country inn there."

"That's a great idea!" I responded. "I'm sure people will love to stay in a quaint old place like that!"

"Yeah," Matt said with a grin. "And hopefully those same people will decide to rent horses and buy honey and Mill Valley Vineyard grape juice, jelly, and wine while they're here."

"I'm sure they will," I said. "It'll be so great to vacation in the park. People will never want to leave."

Matt lowered his eyes. "I know I don't want to."

"You're leaving?" I asked, feeling disappointment wash over me.

"Tonight. I have to," Matt explained. "I've already

missed way too much school at home. And now that my grandfather's up and around . . ." His voice trailed off.

"I understand," I said.

"I'll be back for all my vacations," Matt said. "So we can see each other then."

"That's true," I said. "Thanksgiving's only a couple of weeks away."

"Hey, yeah!" Matt said, his face brightening. He paused. "Sophie, I'll never forget everything you did." He reached into his pocket of his jean jacket. "Here, this is for you." He took out a small package wrapped in purple paper.

"What is it?" I asked, surprised.

"Go on, open it," he urged.

I tore open the paper. Inside was a tiny silver horse pendant on a chain.

"I love it!" I said. "It's beautiful." I slipped the chain over my head. "Thank you, Matt."

Matt smiled at me, his green eyes sparkling. "Thank you, Sophie." He leaned over and kissed my cheek. I hugged him, and he hugged me back.

"Hey, let's go for one more ride before you have to leave," I suggested.

"Well, okay, but are you sure you can ride like that?" Matt asked, indicating the cast on my arm.

"No problem," I said with a grin. "You're not talking to some amateur here, you know, Matt. Remember, I happen to be one of the only two people in the world who can ride Blizzard."

"Yeah, I've been meaning to ask you for days now. How *did* you do that?" Matt asked as we took off toward the stable.

I grinned. "It's my own special trick. But I'll teach it to you," I replied, starting to hum.

ALL-NEW! ALL-EXCITING! ALL GIRL-FRIENDLY!
GRAND PRIZE: $500 WORTH OF CAMPING EQUIPMENT. 50 RUNNERS-UP: GIRLS R.U.L.E. T-SHIRTS.

No purchase necessary. For complete details see below. To enter the drawing, fill in the information below and return it to:

girls R.U.L.E.

375 Hudson Street, Dept. JH
New York, New York 10014

NAME_____

ADDRESS_____

CITY_____ STATE_____

ZIP_____ PHONE #_____

Mail this entry form or a plain 3" x 5" piece of paper postmarked no later than 12/31/98.

1. On an official entry form or a plain 3" x 5" piece of paper print or type your name, address, and telephone number and mail your entry to **GIRLS R.U.L.E. SWEEPSTAKES**, THE BERKLEY PUBLISHING GROUP, DEPT. JH, 375 Hudson Street, New York, New York 10014. No purchase necessary.

2. Entries must be postmarked no later than December 31, 1998. Not responsible for lost or misdirected mail. Enter as often as you wish, but each entry must be mailed separately.

3. The winner will be determined in a random drawing on January 8, 1999. The winner will be notified by mail.

4. This drawing is open to all U.S. and Canadian (excluding Quebec) residents age 13 and over. If a resident of Canada is selected in the drawing, he or she may be required to correctly answer a skill question to claim a prize. Void where prohibited by law. Employees (and their families) of Penguin Putnam Inc., Pearson, plc and their respective affiliates, retailers, distributors, advertising, promotion and production agencies are not eligible.

5. Taxes are the sole responsibility of the prize-winner. The name and likeness of the winner may be used for promotional purposes. The winner will be required to sign and return a statement of eligibility and liability/promotional release within 14 days of notification.

6. No substitution of the prize is permitted. The prize is non-transferable.

7. In the event there is an insufficient number of entries, the sponsor reserves the right not to award the prize.

8. For the name of the prize-winner, send a self-addressed, stamped envelope to GIRLS R.U.L.E. SWEEPSTAKES, Dept. JH, The Berkley Publishing Group, 375 Hudson Street, New York, NY 10014.

9. The Berkley Publishing Group and its affiliates, successors and assigns are not responsible for any claims or injuries of contestants in connection with the contest or prizes.